"I believe our child will want me."

Raff's voice was harsh.

Bryna paled. "What on earth are you talking about? What child?"

Raff's eyes were steely. "The one you're carrying. My child. I called your doctor, Bryna. He confirmed my suspicions."

"Look, Raff. I meant what I said yesterday. It's over between us." Again she lied, feeling miserable. "Anyway, you already have two children. You don't need mine."

"Do you want this child?" he asked fiercely.

"Yes," she shouted, tears glistening in her eyes.

"Well, so do I," he told her softly.

"But why?" She wrenched away from him. "You can have children with any woman, whereas I—" She broke off abruptly. "This baby is mine."

"Ours," he corrected. "And no matter what other plans you may have made, you're going to marry me!"

CAROLE MORTIMER, one of our most popular—and prolific—English authors, began writing in the Harlequin Presents series in 1979. She now has more than forty top-selling romances to her credit and shows no signs whatever of running out of plot ideas. She writes strong traditional romances with a distinctly modern appeal, and her winning way with characters and romantic plot twists has earned her an enthusiastic audience worldwide.

Books by Carole Mortimer

HARLEQUIN PRESENTS

HARLEQUIN SIGNATURE EDITION

Don't miss any of our special offers. Write to us at the following address for information on our newest releases.

Harlequin Reader Service
901 Fuhrmann Blvd., P.O. Box 1397, Buffalo, NY 14240
Canadian address: P.O. Box 603,
Fort Erie, Ont. L2A 5X3

CAROLE MORTIMER

after the loving

Harlequin Books

TORONTO • NEW YORK • LONDON
AMSTERDAM • PARIS • SYDNEY • HAMBURG
STOCKHOLM • ATHENS • TOKYO • MILAN

For John,
Matthew and Joshua

Harlequin Presents first edition October 1987
ISBN 0-373-11019-7

Original hardcover edition published in 1987
by Mills & Boon Limited

CHAPTER ONE

'CONGRATULATIONS, Bryna,' Frank Stapleton beamed at her. 'By my calculations you're just nine weeks pregnant.'

The fingers that had been rebuttoning her blouse after the examination began to shake. Pregnant? My God, she thought, that possibility hadn't even occurred to her when she had made the appointment to see the man who had been her doctor ever since she came to London eight years ago. *Pregnant?* She couldn't be!

'I'll give you an initial prescription for the usual vitamins,' her doctor continued briskly. 'I'm sure you can be relied upon to be sensible during these early weeks—good diet, a healthy amount of exercise, are very important at this stage. You——'

'Are you sure?' Her voice broke with the tension his diagnosis had put her under. 'I meant,' she hurried on at his frowning look, 'I always thought—well, I wouldn't want to—to tell anyone unless I'm one hundred per cent sure.' She hoped she didn't look—or sound—as anxious as she felt to have him tell her he couldn't be *completely* sure that his diagnosis was the right one. At any other time in her life she would have been overjoyed with the news, and she knew Frank was aware of that, but she *couldn't* be pregnant *now*.

Frank gave her a reassuring smile. 'Believe me,

Bryna, there's no doubt. It's amazing how many women ask me the same thing when I tell them the good news,' he teased. 'Even though they're usually pretty certain of what my diagnosis will be before they come here.'

The last was said cajolingly, but she *hadn't* known, hadn't even guessed that the results of the tests the doctor had taken the previous week would reveal that this was the reason her body had decided to play tricks on her. All the experts claimed that emotional tension could cause the same result, and God knows she had been through enough of that recently!

'Now as soon as you can I want you to get along and see a good obstetrician,' her doctor advised. 'I can give you the name of one if you would prefer——'

'There's no rush, is there?' She was still too numb to think about things like that.

'I shouldn't leave it too long, Bryna,' the doctor smiled, moving to sit on the edge of his desk. 'You and the baby will need the best of care during the next seven months.'

Pregnant. It still didn't seem real to her. It couldn't be happening to her *now*!

She studiously finished buttoning her blouse so that the doctor shouldn't see that he was more pleased by the news than she was, and picked up her bag ready to leave once she was fully dressed, a blush darkening her cheeks as the doctor raised surprised brows. She gave him a quick smile. 'Unlike those other ladies who came to you, I have to admit to being a little—surprised,' she revealed shakily. 'You must realise why.' She looked at him dazedly.

'Of course I do,' he patted her hand. 'And as soon as you're feeling a little less shocked I want you to give me a call so that we can talk about that. The only thing you need to know now is that you're in excellent health and I'm sure you're going to have a perfectly normal pregnancy.'

Nothing had been normal in her life the last few weeks, and her pregnancy could only make things worse. Its existence already did that.

'Thank you.' She swallowed hard. 'I am a little dazed,' she admitted tremulously. 'I—I'll call you later today,' she added shakily, clutching her bag in front of her. As if a few hours were going to make any difference to the shock she had just received!

Frank nodded, smiling warmly. 'I'm sure you're bursting to tell someone your good news.'

By 'someone' she knew he meant the baby's father. And that was where the problem lay.

'Yes,' she gave a tight smile. 'Well, thank you, and——'

'Don't thank me, Bryna,' he gave her a teasing smile. 'I had nothing to do with this miracle, you and the baby's father managed this all on your own!'

The trembling hadn't stopped by the time she had walked through the reception area and waiting-room, across the car park, unlocked her car door, and sat inside, her head resting on the steering-wheel.

Pregnant! Years ago she had dreamt about this day, of knowing her child was growing inside her.

Then her parents had broken the news that, owing to an emergency operation during puberty, she would probably never be able to have a child of her own.

It had been a bitter blow, days of crying, weeks of cursing fate for doing this to her, months of self-recrimination as she tried desperately to convince herself she was still a woman worth loving, years of telling herself she could still live a full life, her years as a model doing a lot for her self-esteem. And now, somehow, when she had only fleetingly glimpsed the happiness she could have, she found she was pregnant. With Raff's child.

Raff. He was the last person she could tell about the life they had created between them.

She put her hand protectively on her stomach. Her child.

Dear God, how she wanted it!

But she would lose Raff if she had the baby.

She was losing him anyway.

The last thought came unbidden, but she knew it was the truth even as she tried to deny it. Each day Raff faded a little more away from her, until eventually he would tell her it was over between them. She was only surprised he hadn't already done so; she had lasted much longer than his affairs usually did.

It still surprised her to realise she was the mistress of Raff Gallagher, a man who wielded much power in the City, both monetarily and personality-wise. The first moment she had seen him she had known he was a power to be reckoned with. But she certainly hadn't expected to become his mistress within a matter of days!

He wouldn't want this child she carried, she had no doubt of that. Raff had made it clear from the first that he was offering her no more than any of the other women he had had in his life the last ten years: passion and consideration, and the truth when he no longer felt either of them for her any more.

How could she tell the man who had made it clear he offered no commitment that they had made the biggest commitment of all, that of forming another life from their desire for each other? Once again she acknowledged that she couldn't tell him. Which gave her only a matter of weeks with him before the child physically began to show on her slender figure.

Why bother to count in weeks when she knew Raff could end it in days? Maybe even today.

'So will you talk to Daddy about it?'

Bryna blinked at the pretty girl who sat opposite her at the restaurant table. Lunch had been the last thing she had felt like after leaving the doctor's surgery, but she had promised to have lunch with Kate, and somehow she had managed to drive herself to the restaurant. How, she didn't know, not recalling the drive here at all, but she had already been seated at the table when Kate had breezed into the room five minutes ago, her hair a mass of glossy black curls, grey eyes gleaming with determination.

It was that gleam of determination that warned Bryna she had better be more on her guard and pay

closer attention to what Kate was saying; this young
lady could be deviously charming when she chose to
be! And lack of attention when Kate's eyes were
gleaming like this could have dire results. This
young lady could be every bit as manipulative as her
father when she was set on a course of action.

'Talk to him about what?' Bryna prompted
guardedly, listening intently now.

Irritation flickered in the dark grey depths.
'What's the matter with you today, Bryna? You
haven't heard a word I've said since I arrived!'

Bryna gave a half-smile as Kate displayed
another characteristic of her father: impatience
with anyone who didn't pay complete attention to
what concerned them at any given moment. In the
father it was part of his strength of character, in this
eighteen-year-old girl it appeared merely petulant.
But she didn't doubt Kate would be every inch the
matriarch in her later years.

'Sorry. I—I've had a busy morning,' she dismissed with a shrug.

'Hm,' Kate gave her a censorious look. 'Well, I'd
like you to talk to Daddy on my behalf about the
idea of my sharing a flat with Brenda next term.'

Bryna's brow cleared at the explanation. 'I
thought you'd already discussed it with your father
and he'd said no,' she returned drily, knowing all
about the conversation between father and daughter, also knowing the outcome would be inevitable.

'Not a definite no-more-discussion-on-the-
subject no.' Kate sat forward eagerly. 'I'm sure that
if you told him you think it's a good idea he might be
more—open-minded.'

Bryna wasn't sure she did think it was a good idea. Oh, she understood Kate's wish to leave the home she had shared with her family the last eighteen years, but she wasn't altogether sure Kate was up to setting up home on her own just yet, especially with Brenda Sanders.

Kate had become friends with the other girl when she had started college the previous term, but Brenda seemed to have a different boy in tow each time they met, and the one time Bryna had been to the flat Kate proposed sharing it had been very untidy, with a sleepy-eyed, completely naked young man emerging from Brenda's bedroom. That way of life might be Brenda's choice, but for all her outward sophistication she was sure Kate was still very much an innocent. And her father would like her to remain that way a little while longer!

'I don't think my opinion, favourable or otherwise, would make the slightest difference to his decision,' she told the younger girl coolly, sipping her mineral water, having realised just in time before she ordered her drink from the waiter that she shouldn't really drink alcohol in her condition.

'Oh, but I'm sure—— Oh,' Kate broke off as realisation dawned. 'You aren't saying that your affair with Daddy is almost over?'

Candour, cruelly blunt or otherwise, was something neither of the Gallagher children lacked, neither Paul at twenty, or his young sister Kate. It was something Bryna had been made aware of the first time Raff had introduced her to his two children from his very young marriage and they had asked why she and Raff didn't just live together and have an open affair, assuring them that they were both adult enough to accept the situation.

They might well be, but neither she nor Raff had wanted that close a relationship, she because she liked having her own home and independence, Raff because he never became that intimate with the women he was involved with, and both of them were happy to continue as they were. Or they had been.

'I don't believe it,' Kate dismissed before she could answer her. 'You and Daddy have been together for over six months now; that's at least three months longer than any of the others!'

Tact and diplomacy seemed to be traits the Gallagher children *hadn't* received when virtues were being given out!

Bryna was well aware of the fact that her affair with Raff had lasted twice as long as they usually did, just as she had been aware of his increasing irritability the last month or so, knowing it was only a matter of time now before he ended things between them.

Until today, until an hour ago, she had been grateful for each extra *day* she had lasted than his other women; now she knew she would have no choice but to end things herself if he didn't do it soon.

'All the more reason for him to feel enough is enough,' she gave a tight smile.

'I don't believe it,' his daughter scoffed. 'Paul and I have been laying bets on how soon he would marry you!'

Bryna gave the younger girl a pitying look. 'You

should both know better than that.'

Grey eyes, so much like her father's it was unnerving, looked Bryna over speculatively. 'I somehow never expected the woman to turn *Daddy* down when he finally decided to take the plunge again.'

She turned away. 'One has to be asked in order to give a refusal.'

'You're so beautiful, Daddy is sure to ask you soon,' the younger girl said with certainty.

As if beauty had anything to do with it! Oh, she was well aware of her own looks, she had to be in the profession she had chosen to enter on leaving school eight years ago. She knew how well her long mane of white-blonde straight hair and wide, dark-lashed, violet-coloured eyes photographed, not to mention the slender length of her body.

Her looks had been her stock-in-trade for six years, and could have continued to do so for many years after that, but two years ago she had decided to open her own modelling agency, where her looks and appearance were still very important, but she no longer had to watch everything she ate, or look anxiously in the mirror each morning as she searched for those tell-tale lines on her face that would tell her the choice was no longer hers to make.

It had been a successful move, both financially and personally, and she had also met Raff through the agency. But while her beauty might have attracted his attention initially, it certainly wasn't enough to hold his interest for any length of time; there had been too many beautiful women before her for her to ever believe that.

'I don't think so, Kate,' she dismissed as gently as she could, liking the young girl for all her brashness. How could she not like the daughter who looked so much like the man she loved!

No ties, no commitment, they had said at the start of their affair, and Bryna had meant to keep to those rules. But it had been impossible for her not to fall in love with Raff, although she had taken care not to let him even guess at the emotion, knowing it would precipitate the end of their relationship. She had broken all the rules, but Raff had kept to every one of them, and she had no illusions why.

Would the child she carried look like him as Kate did? They were both tall, so the child was sure to inherit that trait from one of them, but Raff was so dark against her blondeness, and surely that would be the more dominant of the two. How strange to look at her child and see Raff in every glance!

'Bryna? Bryna!' Kate repeated impatiently at her second lapse into unattentiveness. 'Are you sure? I mean——'

'I'm sure. And I accept it,' she huskily assured the young girl. 'Now let's order lunch, shall we?' she added briskly as the waiter approached their table. 'It hasn't happened yet, and until it does we can enjoy each other's company.'

She was well aware that when her affair with Raff ended he wouldn't be the only one to leave her life, that, fond as she had become of Kate and Paul, they could hardly keep up a friendship with one of their father's ex-mistresses!

Kate gave her a frowning look once they had

ordered their meal. 'You don't seem exactly heartbroken.'

Bryna gave rueful grimace. 'Would it do any good if I screamed and shouted?'

'Well ... no,' Kate admitted moodily. 'But it might make *you* feel better.'

'Believe me, it wouldn't,' Bryna drawled.

'You're always so cool and controlled,' the girl rebuked. 'Don't you care for Daddy at all?'

Her heart felt heavy at the irony of that. 'I don't think you really want me to answer that——'

'But I do,' Kate insisted earnestly. 'Daddy tells me that I shouldn't even think about going to bed with someone unless I'm absolutely sure I'm in love with them, and yet Daddy isn't in love with the women he goes to bed with.'

Bryna picked uninterestedly at the prawns she had chosen as her appetiser. 'It doesn't seem very fair, does it?' she acknowledged, her cheeks pale beneath their light dusting of blusher.

'He told me there's a certain type of woman a man would never contemplate marrying,' Kate added with a bitchiness unusual for her.

Bryna swallowed hard, recognising the accusation for what it was. Except that she knew Raff didn't mean her. He had been her first and only lover.

After her parents had told her she could never have a child she had deliberately set out to attract men to the sensuous sway of her body, always drawing back before any physical commitment had been made, believing they would realise she wasn't a complete woman if they ever made love to her. By the time she realised that wasn't true she had earned herself the reputation of being icy and aloof. And the ice hadn't begun to melt until she met Raff. If he had been surprised to find her virginity intact he had never said so.

The bitchy comment hadn't been worthy of Kate, with her forthright manner and lack of guile. Bryna guessed that the girl was fond of her too, and would miss her when the time came.

'He was right,' she told the younger girl.

Only six years separated them in age, and yet at eighteen Bryna had already been mature beyond her years, scarred by what she believed to be her inadequacy. God, how she wished she could share the life growing within her with someone! Preferably Raff.

But that was out of the question. Her parents, then. She didn't doubt for a moment that they would be overjoyed by the news, whether she had a husband or not; as Bryna was an only child they had given up any idea of ever becoming grandparents. Maybe instead of telephoning them she would go up to Scotland at the weekend and tell them in person; the look on their faces might be worth the long journey!

'I'm sorry, Bryna.' Kate gave a self-disgusted sigh at her intention to wound. 'You aren't what Daddy meant at all.' She picked up her fork to eat her salmon. 'I'm disappointed, that's all,' she grimaced. 'I thought you would make a great stepmother.'

Raff had lost his wife, and Kate and Paul their mother, over ten years ago, but Raff gave the impression that the marriage he had entered into at only eighteen had ceased to be a complete success years before that. But both parents were devoted to the children, and while their marriage didn't exactly sparkle it hadn't been unpleasant either.

Paul and Kate obviously had very warm memories of their mother, and it warmed Bryna to know that Kate, at least, would have had no objection to her taking that place in her father's life. If the situation had ever arisen. Which it never would.

'Thank you,' she accepted briskly. 'Now, as a friend, would you hurry up and eat your lunch; I have to get back to work.' She smiled brightly in the face of Kate's pain at the deliberate snub; she couldn't allow Kate to live under the misapprehension that there would ever be a happy-ever-after between Raff and herself. Raff was thirty-nine years old, with a grown-up family, and the thought of having to go through night-time feeds, teething, crawling, walking, the terrible-twos, and so on and so on, with another child, would throw even the self-confidently arrogant Raff Gallagher into a panic! It threw *her* into a panic!

Who would have guessed when she had walked into a restaurant very similar to this one six short months ago that this would happen?

She had been meeting Courtney Stevens, to discuss the use of six of her models to promote a new line he was introducing to his chain of fashion stores throughout Europe and America for the winter. He had proved every bit as charming as the advertising agency she was working with had told her he was.

Or warned her. She and Janet Parker had worked together before, and when the cynical Janet described a man as 'charming' it was like any other woman saying he was lethally attractive!

Courtney Stevens—or Court, as he had insisted she call him as they introduced themselves—was a blond giant of a man with a devilish charm glinting in deep blue eyes that were guaranteed to seduce even the most hardened of women. Bryna was charmed almost from the first moment, almost forgetting what she was there for as he deftly centred the conversation on her rather than the business she had come here to discuss.

'We have to decide what models you would like to use,' she had finally laughingly protested.

'Well, we're going to use the family pile,' he dismissed drily. 'For some reason my father bought himself a manor house in Kent and left it to me in his will; I've never had reason to use it until now. So as it means the crew will have to stay overnight down there, how about making one of the models a tall violet-eyed silver-blonde?' He looked at her expectantly.

She couldn't possibly feel insulted by the intimacy of the suggestion, and she laughed huskily. 'I no longer work as a model myself.'

'Couldn't you make this the exception?' His large hand covered her much slenderer one.

Her eyes glowed. 'I'm afraid not.'

'No?' He looked as if she had dealt him a wounding blow. 'Then how about joining me for——'

'Would you like to introduce us, Court?' interrupted a harshly rasping voice.

Court frowned his irritation up at the other man.

'Not now, Raff,' he protested.

'Exactly now,' the other man drawled.

'Bryna, Raff Gallagher. Raff, Bryna Fairchild,' Court made the introductions in a disgruntled voice. 'A friend of mine,' he told the other man pointedly.

'I'm glad to meet you, Miss Fairchild.' The man, who until that moment had only been a dark blue tailored suit, she could see out of the corner of her eye, and a rasping voice, lowered himself into the chair beside her.

For some reason just the sound of his voice as he cut in on their conversation had made her reluctant to look at him before, and as she glanced at him now she knew the reason why; it was like the moon eclipsing the sun. Court was the sun, open and uncomplicated, and Raff Gallagher was the moon, dark with secretive depths he allowed no one to enter.

She told herself she was being imaginative, and yet piercing grey eyes seemed to look into her very soul and see all that was Bryna Fairchild.

Raff couldn't be called handsome, his features were too rugged for that, and yet he had something else that was even more effective, a compelling quality that overshadowed and obliterated every other man but him.

He appeared to be the same age as Court, in his late thirties, and yet the years had left their mark in the cynical twist of his mouth, the hardness of his eyes, and the grey wings of hair over each temple.

And from the moment she looked at him Court

Stevens ceased to be anything but an attractively pleasant client.

'Mr Gallagher,' she greeted him coolly.

'Please call me Raff,' he invited gruffly. 'I have every intention of calling you Bryna.'

Whether she liked it or not! she acknowledged ruefully. Of course she realised who he was now; anyone who was in business and hadn't heard of Raff Gallagher was either a fool or doomed to fail. And she hoped she was neither of those things. This man was Midas, anything he touched, from property to industry, turning to gold.

'Raff, why don't you get lost?' Court invited irritably. 'Bryna and I have some business to discuss. Not that sort of business, you fool,' he admonished as the other man raised disbelieving brows in Bryna's direction. 'Bryna runs the Fairchild Agency.'

The dark brow cleared. 'I've heard of it,' Raff drawled, turning to Bryna. 'I apologise for the assumption I made just now.'

Being a model, Bryna had received her fair share of insults over erroneous assumptions of what her profession actually entailed, but never before had a man presumed *that* about her without knowing a thing about her!

She turned to Court Stevens with frosty eyes. 'I really do have to go,' she snapped. 'Perhaps you could give me a call and we could get together to discuss this another time.' She was probably walking away from a contract that could mean even bigger things for her agency if Court Stevens was pleased with the work they did for him this time, but she wasn't going to stay around and be insulted by a man who acted as if he owned half of London— and probably did!

'Now look what you've done!' Court turned accusing eyes on the other man. 'Will you just get out of here?'

It was testament to how deep the friendship was between the two men that Raff Gallagher didn't take exception to the way Court had been trying to get rid of him ever since he had interrupted them. But at that moment Bryna was too angry to care how close the two men were, as she stood up to leave.

'Please stay, Miss Fairchild,' Raff Gallagher drawled as he stood up, the formality deliberate, she was sure. 'And please accept my apology for interrupting the two of you. Game of golf tomorrow, Court?'

'OK,' Court sighed unenthusiastically. 'But you're starting with a handicap.'

'Don't I always,' the other man mocked. 'Miss Fairchild,' he nodded dismissively before strolling across the restaurant to join two men at a table who had obviously been waiting for him.

'He always wins, too,' muttered Court. 'Sit down, Bryna. Please,' he persuaded.

She did so slowly, pointedly turning her chair so that she didn't have to look at Raff Gallagher.

'We became friends in our first week of boarding school after he bowled me out at cricket and I hit him with my cricket bat in the changing room,' Court sighed. 'I broke his nose.'

Bryna had noticed that slight bump on the

hawklike nose, laughing softly now as she envisaged the two little boys glaring at each other across
a cricket bat, both taking their aggression at being
away from home out on the other. 'Stranger
meetings have formed just as strong a friendship,
I'm sure,' she teased.

Court smiled, his eyes brimming with laughter.
'It wasn't the fight that caused the friendship,' he
assured her. 'What did that was the fact that Raff
told everyone he'd fallen over and hit his nose. If he
hadn't I would have been expelled in my first week
of school!'

Two little boys who had bonded a lifetime
friendship through resentment and pain. Maybe
Raff Gallagher did have some redeeming qualities
after all. One just had to dig deep to find them!

She made a point of not looking his way as she
and Court got down to the serious business of
discussing the models. Nevertheless, she was aware
of the exact moment Raff Gallagher stood up to
approach their table before leaving.

Grey eyes delved into her soul a second time.
'We'll meet again, Miss Fairchild,' he murmured as
he bent over the hand he had lifted to his mouth, his
lips cool and yet moist.

'Give me a chance, Raff!' Court complained.

His friend chuckled huskily. 'The choice will be
Bryna's,' he said softly, meeting her gaze once again
with compelling intensity before taking his leave.

'It's a no contest,' groaned Court resignedly. 'It
always is.'

'I can assure you Mr Gallagher holds no interest
for me,' Bryna dismissed primly.

When she got back to her office a box containing a single red rose lay on her desk. There was no card with it, but she guessed that it wasn't from Court; he was the type of man who would sign his name with a flourish to the accompanying card if he found a woman attractive enough to send her flowers.

Half an hour later two more roses arrived, half an hour after that another three, then another three, and another three, until by four-thirty she had the round dozen.

Her secretary/receptionist, Gilly, was agog to know who had sent them. When the man himself arrived at five o'clock neither woman was in any doubt as to who the sender had been. When Raff courteously invited Bryna out to dinner she had breathlessly accepted, her earlier antagonism forgotten; she had never met anyone quite like this man before.

She still hadn't met anyone like him, and even when he was long gone from her life, she knew she would never meet anyone like him again.

CHAPTER TWO

'KATE tells me the two of you had lunch together today,' Raff said enquiringly as he sat down opposite her.

Bryna met his gaze guardedly, her heart skipping its usual beat as she looked at him, still affected, even after six months of knowing him intimately, by that compelling power that surrounded him. Tonight, dressed in black evening suit and snowy white shirt, he appeared even more devastating than usual.

'That's right, we did,' she confirmed coolly, wondering where the conversation was leading to.

Raff gave an inclination of his head, his mouth twisted into a rueful smile. 'She seems slightly annoyed with you.'

She and Kate had parted a little stiffly outside the restaurant, the younger girl seeming to blame Bryna for the fact that her father hadn't fallen in love with her!

Bryna shrugged. 'She hoped I would talk to you about her moving in with Brenda next term,' she told him truthfully.

His eyes became suddenly flinty. 'And what did you tell her?'

She maintained her calm poise in the face of his obvious displeasure. 'What do you think I told her?' she drawled.

Raff relaxed slightly, his long length stretched out comfortably in the armchair. 'I think you agree with me, that young lady is *not* the choice of flatmate I want for Kate.'

And what Raff wanted he invariably got, Bryna had found these last months. She was a prime example of that, in the past having been able to freeze off even the most ardent of men, and yet she and Raff had been lovers within days of their meeting. And far from feeling inadequate as she had always imagined she would, she had felt complete for the first time in her life! It had been the same every time they made love.

'Perhaps not Brenda,' she agreed. 'But I think Kate is determined to get a place of her own, and she is over eighteen——'

'I think I know what's best for my children, Bryna,' he bit out cuttingly, standing up abruptly. 'We should be going now,' he added curtly. 'At the moment we're politely late, any later and we may as well not bother!'

Despite the fact that the dig about their lateness was aimed at her she wanted to say 'then let's not bother!' She wanted to be in his arms tonight, close to him in the only way he allowed any woman to be close to him. She had long ago ceased to be upset by the way he cut her out of showing any interest in his children's activities; it was far from the first time he had done so. To her it only served to emphasise the transient role she played in his life.

And because of the child she herself carried inside her she didn't suggest they miss the party, but slipped her arms into the coat he held out for her, the suede soft and supple against her body. 'I'm sure Court won't mind our tardiness,' she shrugged lightly.

She wished he would smile, because it completely transformed his face when he did, alleviating some of the harshness, lending warmth to eyes the colour of slate, the harshness of his mouth softening as deep grooves were etched into the leanness of his cheeks.

Instead he nodded tersely. 'After all these years Court has come to expect my rudeness,' he said drily. 'I wouldn't want to disappoint him!'

The two men were still the unlikeliest couple to have found such an enduring friendship that Bryna had ever met, Raff being hard where Court was gentle, Raff blunt to the point of rudeness where Court was always kind. Bryna had even wondered, when loving Raff hurt too badly, why it couldn't have been Court she fell in love with that day. But she hadn't, and so the two of them had become friends instead.

'What did the doctor say?'

Her smile faded as she looked up at Raff with startled eyes. 'Sorry?' she frowned, her hands shaking slightly as she held her coat around her as they braved the icy-cold early December winds to go out to the waiting Jaguar, the sudden chill not leaving her body even as Raff turned on the ignition and the burst of warm air filled the interior.

'You told me last night that the doctor was going to tell you the results of your tests today,' he explained raspingly. 'You did keep the appointment, didn't you?' The lights on the dashboard illuminated his frown.

'Yes, of course.' Bryna huddled down into the collar of her coat, the chill seeming to have permeated her bones.

She inwardly bemoaned the fact that the intimacy of their relationship told Raff without words exactly when her body had failed her. She had assured him that it occasionally happened, although he had been aware that it never had in their previous four months together. When it happened again he had been the one to urge her to consult a doctor.

'I'm anaemic, that's all,' she evaded. 'It can have that effect. The doctor has given me some vitamins,' she added truthfully.

Raff gave her a probing look. 'You do look a little pale,' he conceded.

She looked pale because she was still suffering from the shock of knowing she was pregnant; even the call to her parents telling them she would be home for the weekend hadn't made the baby she carried seem more real to her. She was sure there would be visible signs of it soon enough, but at the moment, with her body still so slender, and no ill-effects such as morning sickness to cope with, she couldn't help questioning the accuracy of the doctor's diagnosis.

Except that she felt different emotionally, filled with a tranquillity and inner peace she had thought never to know. Maternal instinct had previously only been an expression to her, but now she knew exactly what it was, the completely unselfish love for a human being you just *knew* was inside you despite there being no visible signs of its existence.

'Warmer now?' Raff cut in on her musings. 'You seem a little distracted this evening,' he frowned as she raised questioning brows. 'You shivered earlier, I wondered if you were warmer now,' he explained.

'Fine,' she gave him a dreamy smile. 'Isn't it a lovely evening?'

'It's been raining most of the day and they forecast sleet for tonight,' he drawled derisively.

Bryna blushed self-consciously. 'I happen to like rain,' she defended, her golden bubble firmly burst.

'And sleet?' Raff arched dark brows.

She realised it was ridiculous to expect Raff Gallagher to act like a giddy lover, but sometimes she wished he wasn't quite so controlled and cynical all the time. It would be nice to sometimes relax with him completely and show him how much she cared.

But it was impossible with a man as armoured against the softer feelings as Raff was, and she knew it was only the child she carried inside her that made her hunger for that closeness now.

'No,' she conceded ruefully. 'But maybe this bad weather is an indication that we're going to have a white Christmas this year.'

'And then you wouldn't be able to get to your parents' house for the holiday,' he rasped.

'No.' She was tempted to tell him she wouldn't mind that too much as she was going home this weekend anyway, but on their way to a party didn't seem the appropriate time to tell him that.

'Of course you're welcome to spend Christmas

with us if anything goes wrong with your plans,' he invited smoothly.

If he had issued that invitation a few weeks ago she would have been tempted to accept no matter how out of place she felt at the time, but he hadn't suggested it before, neither had he shown any sign of displeasure that they wouldn't be spending the holiday together. 'I don't think so, thank you,' she refused lightly. 'Christmas is a time for families, isn't it?'

His jaw tightened. 'Yes, I suppose so.'

The drive from Raff's house to Court's apartment was a short one, and Bryna was relieved to escape the suddenly icy atmosphere that had developed in the car after her refusal. She didn't know what Raff was so annoyed about—his invitation had lacked warmth, to say the least! And it was also a little late in coming, when he knew she had made her plans weeks ago.

'My favourite lady!' Court greeted her warmly as soon as they were admitted to his apartment, kissing her lightly on the lips as he took her coat himself. 'I thought you were never going to get here,' he grinned at her. 'It's Raff's fault you're late, of course——'

'Of course,' the other man drawled coolly.

'Only because you knew the sole reason I arranged this party at all was so that I could ask Bryna to dance and hold her in my arms for a while!' Court challenged firmly. 'Bryna?'

'I'd love to dance,' she accepted laughingly. The lounge of Court's apartment was completely cleared of furniture, a dozen or so couples moving sensuously together in there to the sound of a romantic love song.

'You look lovely tonight.' Court looked down at her appreciatively.

Raff had told her the same thing earlier about the purple dress that made her eyes appear the same colour, but somehow Court's compliment seemed less perfunctory. Or maybe tonight she was just looking for faults in her relationship with Raff; the pity of it was it was so easy to find them!

Court looked at her searchingly. 'There's a sort of glow to you ... Oh God, I haven't stepped in with my size tens, have I?' he groaned as a blush darkened her cheeks.

'Raff and I came straight here, if that's what you mean,' she told him. 'I'm afraid it was *my* fault we got here late; I arrived late at Raff's.' Because of the telephone call to her parents, both of them concerned—if delighted!—at her sudden need to go home for the weekend. It had taken her some time to convince them that nothing had gone drastically wrong in her life to warrant the visit.

Court shook his head. 'I'm surprised Raff hasn't told you you work too hard.'

'He has,' she smiled. 'But as he wouldn't tolerate interference in his business neither will I!'

His friend chuckled softly. 'No wonder he finds you so fascinating; all his other women were quite willing to forgo their own plans to pander to his whims!'

'I sometimes wonder if you two love or hate each other!' she mocked.

'Love, of course,' Court drawled. 'Although if

looks could kill I'd be dead now!' he groaned as he glanced over Bryna's shoulder. 'Unless it's you he's upset at? Maybe he really didn't like your being late earlier.'

He hadn't seemed too worried at the time, but from the way he was glaring at the two of them now something had upset him! Perhaps he was still annoyed about Christmas?

He stood beside the bar in the adjoining dining-room, a drink remaining untouched in his hand as Rosemary Chater did her best to attract him to her fiery-haired beauty. For all the notice Raff took of her she might not have been wearing the most low-cut gown Bryna had ever seen, or been wearing that look of open invitation on her beautiful face. Raff's gaze was fixed on Court and Bryna as they moved slowly to the music.

Maybe he really was angry about her refusal to spend Christmas with him and Kate and Paul, but with Christmas only two weeks away he had left the invitation late enough!

She smiled at Court. 'No, I think it's you he's angry with,' she teased him.

'Well, I did beat him at golf today . . .!'

'You didn't!' she laughed disbelievingly; Court had been trying to win a round of golf against Raff ever since she had known the two of them.

'I did,' Court grinned triumphantly. 'Of course his mind didn't seem to be altogether on the game,' he admitted with some reluctance. 'But who's to say I haven't always lost in the past because of pressures of work?'

'I didn't think Raff had any pressures of work

now,' Bryna frowned. Raff had employed a very capable assistant four months ago, and while she might not like Stuart Hillier very much, and found his smooth charm more than a little overpowering, she knew he was good at his job, and that he had taken over a lot of the pressure of the solitary reign over his business empire that Raff had previously refused to relinquish. Everything had seemed to be going so smoothly in that direction the last four months.

Court shrugged. 'How should I know how well it is or isn't going? He never discusses business with me. Maybe it wasn't business worrying him at all, but he certainly had something on his mind.'

Her, and the fact that, despite their agreement that when the affair was over for one, or both, of them, they would admit that honestly, Raff seemed to be having trouble breaking the news to her. Maybe he did care for her in his own distant way and didn't want to hurt her. He might even have guessed at some of the love she felt for him. But she was soon going to have to decide if she walked away from him with some of her pride intact, or if she waited the short time until he ended things once and for all.

'Hey, have I said something I shouldn't?' Court frowned down at her concernedly.

Bryna shook off her mood of depression, knowing he had only confirmed for her what she already knew, smiling brightly to dispel his concern. 'Shall we go and join him before Rosemary falls out of her dress completely?' she suggested drily as the music came to an end.

Court groaned. 'I'm afraid she had herself lined up as next in line to share his bed before he met you.'

And like a vulture the other woman was now circling, waiting for the affair to end, trying to give it a helping hand if she could! And she was certainly going all out to do that at the moment.

From the first Bryna had found the world of cynicism, bitchiness, and self that Raff inhabited a little overwhelming, although she was hardened to a certain degree herself from her years as a top-class model. But almost every woman she met clearly let her, and Raff, know that they wanted him too, only the fact that he showed no interest in returning their attraction giving her comfort during the last months.

Until now. Raff had ceased to look bored by Rosemary Chater, in fact as Court and Bryna moved to join the other couple he led the other woman on to the dance floor, seeming to enjoy the way her body instantly melded to every contour of his.

'She can only cause trouble if you let her,' Court spoke quietly at Bryna's side, also watching the other couple with narrowed eyes.

Bryna turned to him with a grateful smile. 'Then I won't let her.'

He raised blond brows. 'Is it as easy to dismiss as that?'

Easy? She *hated* the way the other woman moved against Raff with deliberate seductiveness, but what could she do about it when Raff was enjoying it? She wasn't a fool, to make a scene about what was, for all the sensuousness of movement, just a dance; she knew that would be the surest way to drive Raff away from her. He hated scenes—he had once told her his wife had caused several before the two of them decided to live together but go their separate ways, to have their own lovers.

'No, it isn't easy,' she gave Court a tight smile. 'Why don't we go through and help ourselves to some of that lovely supper you've laid out in the other room?' It was almost ten o'clock and she hadn't eaten anything since lunchtime. So much for the doctor's confidence that she would maintain a healthy diet!

'Is everything okay between you and Raff?' Court eyed her curiously as she nibbled uninterestedly on a sandwich.

Her eyes were overbright as she looked up at him. '"The Queen is dead. Long live the Queen."' She looked pointedly at Rosemary Chater as she said the latter, too numb to even sound bitter.

Court looked much older when the boyish humour deserted his face. 'Are you sure?'

Her heart was breaking, the tears threatening to cascade down her cheeks—and she was incongruously trying to work out how she could bite into the cold chicken leg she held in her hand, without choking on it! 'Have you ever known him to behave like *that* in front of me before?' She felt sick as she watched Raff nuzzle against the other woman's silky throat.

'Hell!' muttered Court furiously as he followed her stricken gaze. 'I'll go and break them up——'

'No.' Her hand on his arm stopped him. 'Would

you please just get my coat and call a taxi to take me home?'

'I'll take you——'

'This is your party, Court,' she reminded him huskily, no longer able to look at Raff with the other woman. 'The host shouldn't walk out on his guests.' She tried to sound teasing, but to her dismay she just sounded forlorn.

Court's mouth tightened. 'None of this lot cares about that, half of them wouldn't even know I'd gone!'

'I'd really rather go on my own, thank you,' she refused as gently as she could, sure that if she didn't get out of here soon she was going to make an absolute fool of herself.

Court looked as if he were about to argue again, but the pleading in her eyes silenced him. Bryna kept her face averted from the couple dancing as she and Court moved through to the entrance hall to collect her coat.

Raff had done to her what they had always agreed wouldn't happen, publicly humiliated her by turning to another woman when the two of them had arrived here together.

Court put his hands warmly on her shoulders as he came to stand in front of her after helping her on with her coat. 'If you ever need a shoulder to cry on ...' he told her affectionately.

'I know I can call you,' she gave him a wan smile. 'You——'

'Where do you think you're going?' rasped a harsh voice Bryna recognised only too well.

She took a second to regain control before turning

to face Raff, blinking a little uncertainly as she saw the fury blazing in the depths of his eyes. 'I was just about to leave——'

Cool grey eyes turned to Court. 'You too?' Raff bit out coldly.

Court met the challenge in his friend's gaze unflinchingly. 'I wanted to go with her, but Bryna insisted I stay here.'

Raff's mouth twisted. 'Running out on me, Bryna?' he taunted.

'I——'

'Good God, man, what did you expect her to do?' Court exploded. 'Tap you on the shoulder while you were making love to Rosemary to tell you she was leaving!'

'I wasn't making love to her, damn it,' Raff ground out, his hands clenched into fists at his sides.

'Then you were doing a good job of acting as if you were!' his friend accused heatedly.

Grey eyes flickered coldly. 'Bryna?'

She swallowed hard, not enjoying being the bone of contention between the two friends. 'I really think it would be best if I left——'

'Then I'm coming with you,' rasped Raff.

'—and you stayed,' she finished dully. 'There's no point in our both ruining our evening. "The night is still young," and all that,' she added brittlely.

Raff strode purposefully across to grasp her arm in his hand. 'I said I'm coming with you!'

'Maybe she doesn't want to go with you?' Court told him caustically.

His mouth tightened. 'She came with me, she'll leave with me.'

Bryna frowned up at him. Why was he doing this? Couldn't he see this was a perfect way out for him, why drag out their parting any longer than they had to? But she could see by the inflexibility of his jaw that he was determined to leave with her.

'Thank you, Court,' she squeezed his arm reassuringly. 'Raff will take me home.'

'I'll call you tomorrow,' Raff told the other man gratingly.

'Make sure that you do, and that it's nice and early. Otherwise I'll be the one to call you,' Court warned in a controlled voice.

The heating system in the Jaguar was blasting out hot air, and yet Bryna still felt cold. Why was Raff continuing with this? Unless he was going to tell her now that they were finished? As if she didn't already know that!

He accompanied her up to her apartment, neither of them having spoken a word since they left Court's home, Raff's expression harshly forbidding each time she had dared a glance in his direction.

She turned to him once she had unlocked her door. 'I don't think there's any point in your coming in——'

'Of course I'm coming in, Bryna,' his voice was huskily soft, as he pushed the door open for her to precede him inside and closed the door firmly behind him.

Bryna felt nervous in his company, as if this were their first date and they were only a couple of inexperienced teenagers, her hands shaking slightly as she faced him across the lounge. 'Rosemary will be waiting for you——'

'No one is waiting for me,' he told her gruffly, noiselessly crossing the lounge to stand in front of her. 'It's you I want, Bryna.'

Her eyes were wide with disbelief. 'No—you can't mean——'

'I need your fire and passion tonight, Bryna,' he groaned as his head lowered to hers.

'But earlier——'

'I was angry,' he dismissed. 'But I'm not angry any more. Now I just want to feel your silken legs wrapped about me while I bury myself in you!'

Their lovemaking was always different, sometimes fierce, sometimes gentle, sometimes so slow it drove the two of them insane, other times fiercely out of control. And tonight she knew Raff wanted it to be the latter, for both of them to be mindlessly lost in their passion for each other. And she wasn't sure, after what had happened earlier, that she could give him the response he seemed to need.

She swallowed hard. 'Raff, I don't know if I can. I don't——'

'Of course you can.' He melded his body against hers, moving against her provocatively.

Yes, she could, because this would be their farewell. She couldn't go through the pain he had made her endure earlier again, and so they would have this one last night together and then she would tell him it was over between them.

'All right, Raff,' her arms curved up about his neck as she relaxed against him, 'make love to me.'

Asking Raff to make love to her was like standing in the way of a tidal wave, knowing it would knock her completely off her feet, cloud her brain until she couldn't think or feel anything but him!

He was a man who rarely, if ever, lost control, and it took her breath away when he began to throw off their clothes as they stood together in her lounge. Usually they both had a leisurely shower, either apart or together, and then they would go to bed together. She had never known this wildness from him before.

But if he felt differently about their lovemaking tonight so did she, the child inside her, and the knowledge that this would be their last time together, making her own responses as wild as his.

He had a magnificent body, strong and lithe, with not an ounce of superfluous flesh anywhere. And as he stripped off the last of his clothing Bryna was able to see he was already fully aroused.

His hands entangled in her hair as he kissed her deeply, and she squirmed with delight as one of those hands moved to cup the fullness of one of her breasts. She had wondered at the increased sensitivity of her breasts in recent weeks, but now she knew they were making ready for her baby, and as Raff's dark head moved down to allow him to capture one aching nipple into the moist cavern of his mouth she felt as if her child already suckled there.

But the flicking of his tongue and the sharp sting of his teeth were not the movements of a child nourishing, and her legs buckled weakly beneath her, drawing the two of them down on to the carpeted floor.

'Don't move,' Raff instructed gruffly as she would have caressed him.

What followed was the most erotic and tortuous experience of her entire life. Raff kissed her from the top of her head to the soles of her feet, discovering pleasure spots that took her again and again to the edge of the sensual abyss he refused to let her enter, always drawing her back before she could attain release.

Finally she could stand no more, moving above him to take them *both* over the edge as she moved her body in rhythm with his, her nipples knowing the tug of his teeth as she bent above him.

The explosion inside her was greater than anything she had ever known before, and for a brief moment she felt blackness enshroud her, still feeling dizzy as Raff stood up to carry her through to her bedroom.

'That was for us,' he murmured as he gently laid her down between the covers. 'Now this is for you.'

She had barely recovered from the previous onslaught when she felt him intent on arousing her a second time.

He was trying to drive her insane, she decided minutes later, her body writhing and sweat-dampened as she silently begged him to release her from the tortuous frenzy he remorselessly drove her to.

He poised above her, his expression fierce. '*Now* do you believe I want you?' he rasped.

'Yes,' she almost sobbed. 'But please, *please*, Raff,' she let out a shuddering breath of need.

She had been made for him, she decided for what had to be the hundredth time, knowing even as the silken length of him thrust inside her that he would fit perfectly, that he always had.

And then she couldn't think at all, her hips arching to meet his throbbing rhythm, groaning her own shuddering release at the exact moment she felt his warmth inside her.

As partings went, it had to be one of the most soul-shattering on record!

Raff was already in the bathroom showering and shaving when Bryna woke the next morning, falling back against the pillows with a relieved groan as she realised it was Saturday, and her flight wasn't scheduled until later that morning.

Last night had been frightening in its intensity, Raff taking her once more before he allowed her to sleep, and her rest finally that of the almost unconscious, and this morning her body ached from the force of those fierce caresses.

Last night they had been closer than ever before, and Bryna dreaded having to tell Raff she thought it best if they didn't see each other any more. But what real choice did she have?

He was smiling when he came out of the bathroom, freshly shaved, wearing only the black trousers to his suit, although they were a little creased from where they had been left forgotten on the lounge floor all night. His chest was bare and golden, the dark hair there sprinkled even more liberally with grey than at his temples.

He sat on the side of the bed, smoothing back her ice-gold tangle of hair. 'I thought you were going to sleep all day,' he teased indulgently.

She longed to turn her face into that hand, to

shower kisses over his palm, to tell him how much she loved him, of his child that she carried inside her. Instead she drew back from him. 'I'm going up to Scotland today to stay the rest of the weekend with my parents.' It was an effort to keep her gaze on a level with him when his darkened angrily. 'I think we should take that time to accept that it's over between us,' she added in a rush of emotion.

Raff drew in a harsh breath, his hand dropping back to his side. 'What do you mean, it's over?' he rasped abruptly.

Bryna sighed. 'We've both known it for weeks, Raff, so why fool ourselves any longer?'

He stood up forcefully, grey eyes blazing. 'When did you decide this?' he demanded.

She shrugged, sitting up against the pillows. 'I've realised for some time——'

'I meant, when did you decide to visit your parents?' he ground out.

'I telephoned them yesterday afternoon and made the arrangements——'

'So you knew when we met to go out last night?' he accused.

She blinked. 'Yes. But——'

'Then what was last night all about?' His voice rose angrily.

Bryna swallowed hard. 'Goodbye?'

'Good——?' His face darkened thunderously as he grabbed hold of her arms and pulled her up to him so that her face was only inches away from him. 'Look at me and tell me you don't want me any more,' he ordered harshly.

For the sake of her pride she had to do it; she

knew she would never be able to face their child if she allowed their relationship to deteriorate to the stage where they were no longer equal but she was just someone Raff came to when he wanted a willing woman in his arms.

She met his gaze steadily. 'I no longer want you,' she lied.

'Damn you!' he grated forcefully, releasing her so suddenly she fell back on the pillows, watching numbly as he pulled on his clothes. 'Damn you,' he said again before slamming out of the apartment.

With a shuddering sob Bryna's body began to heave in racking waves of agony.

CHAPTER THREE

'ARE you sure, darling?' her mother choked through her tears of happiness. 'The doctors seemed so sure——'

'Mine is just as sure I'm pregnant,' Bryna told her laughingly. Her parents' reaction to her news, the one she had expected from them, had been pure joy! At last she had been able to tell someone, and the happiness of sharing her child with them was all she had thought it would be.

'It's just so incredible!' Her father hugged her, tears in his own deep blue eyes. He was tall and muscular, with hair that was grey now but that had once been the same colour as Bryna's.

'I know,' she laughed again. 'Yesterday I was still too shocked by the news to be able to take it in myself, but before I left this morning I called my doctor and asked him if he could be absolutely certain I was pregnant. I mean, he knows my medical history as well as I do! But he's almost certain the doctors told you there was always the possibility I could conceive, even if that possibility was a remote one.' She looked at them questioningly.

Her mother frowned thoughtfully. 'They seemed pretty convinced you wouldn't——'

'Well, he also said that they know more nowadays than they did then, and that perhaps they really did

46

believe I couldn't conceive. But they were wrong,' she told them happily. 'Because my doctor also told me I should start thinking of names!'

'Oh, darling!' Her mother was crying in earnest now, small and dark, with a plump figure Bryna's father had always maintained was cuddly!

Bryna had only arrived half an hour earlier, but she had been too excited to contain her news until after they had all eaten. She came home to see her parents regularly in the home she had known all her life. Her father owned and ran a ski-school in this lovely part of north-east Scotland.

'No more tears,' she instructed briskly, her face glowing. 'Let's have dinner before it spoils.'

'We should have some wine to celebrate,' her father decided, hesitating suddenly. 'Can you drink wine?' he asked curiously.

'One glass occasionally,' she nodded, smiling. 'And I think this is definitely an "occasion"!'

By the time they were halfway through the meal her father was discussing which schools her unborn child should attend! Bryna just smiled at him indulgently, knowing how much he was enjoying himself in his role of grandfather.

'Really, James,' her mother admonished lightly. 'That will be for Bryna and Mr Gallagher to decide.'

A shadow darkened Bryna's eyes to purple. 'Raff and I are no longer together,' she announced flatly.

She had told her parents all about Raff and the part he played in her life after their first week together, never having kept secrets from them, and knowing they respected the fact that she was old enough to make her own decisions—and her own mistakes, if need be.

Her father frowned. 'I'm not old-fashioned enough to believe, or imply, that the two of you should get married because you're pregnant, but surely he'll want to take some interest in his own child?'

'It's my child, Dad——'

'You haven't told him,' he reproved gently. 'Isn't that a little selfish, lass?'

She blushed. 'He already has two children, why should he want mine?'

'Because——'

'Now, James, this isn't the night for an argument,' her mother cut in determinedly. 'I'm sure Bryna knows what she's doing.'

'But, Mary——'

'Not tonight, James!' her mother bit out, her brown eyes flashing warningly. She might be small and cuddly, but when the occasion warranted it she had a fiery temper that even her husband was in awe of!

Bryna gave a rueful smile, as her father, almost twice her mother's size, subsided into silence.

She hadn't meant to cause any friction between her parents, but she didn't want to talk of Raff this weekend, not when she had managed to avoid thinking of him since setting out for Scotland this morning.

It was a pleasant evening for all of them, making plans, laughingly suggesting the most outrageous names they could think of. A boy's name was already decided in her mind—Rafferty James, after its father and grandfather, but a girl's name was a little harder to decide upon. Maybe because she was already convinced she carried Raff's son.

Once she was alone in the single bed in the room that had remained hers, even though she had left so long ago, it was impossible to banish Raff from her mind any longer, and she allowed the tears of desolation to fall unheeded down her heated cheeks.

Was he with Rosemary, or someone like her, tonight, having put from his mind and his life the woman who had dared to end their affair?

God, how she would love his child, she vowed protectively.

Home to her would always be Scotland, Bryna realised the next day as she trudged through the thick snow with her father to the ski-lodge, greeting several of the ski-instructors by name as they entered the building, most of them having been with her father for years.

She had skied almost from the time she could walk, and she longed now to join the skiers on the white slopes. But she wouldn't selfishly risk her child no matter how she ached for the freedom being on skis gave her, having a feeling very much like flying when the skis moved beneath her and the wind whipped through her hair. Almost like making love to Raff. Almost . . .

'I hope you aren't even thinking about it,' rasped a coldly harsh voice from behind her.

Bryna turned so suddenly the ground tipped on its axis and the image of Raff moved in and out of her focus until there was only darkness.

When she returned to consciousness she found she was lying on the leather couch in her father's office.

Only her stricken gaze moved, her breath catching in a pained gasp as she saw the man standing with his back to the room as he stared out of the window at the mountains. He was dressed more casually than she had ever seen him before, in a thick black sweater and fitted denims, and yet she would know that thick dark hair anywhere, the powerful width of his shoulders, tapered waist, and strong thighs.

Raff really was here, and not a figment of her tormented imagination after all!

She moved to sit up, and the movement attracted Raff's attention; his narrowed grey eyes levelled on her. Bryna determinedly withstood that censorious gaze. 'My father?' she prompted abruptly.

Raff's mouth twisted. 'He had to organise some ski-instructors,' he dismissed. 'Once we'd established that you'd merely fainted he seemed quite happy to leave you in my care.'

No doubt her father saw this as the ideal opportunity for her to tell Raff about their baby! But she wasn't going to take it. 'You introduced yourselves?' She swung her legs to the floor, sitting up properly against the back of the sofa.

Raff turned to her fully, his hands thrust into his denims' pockets. 'It's the usual practice when one man finds another man holding his unconscious daughter in his arms!' he scorned.

A blush darkened her cheeks. 'What are you

doing here?' she snapped, still feeling slightly lightheaded.

'I've thought over what you said yesterday,' he told her. 'And I've decided I don't *want* to accept that it's over between the two of us.'

Bryna frowned warily at the silky softness of his tone. 'I told you, I don't want you any more.'

'So you did,' he nodded. 'But I believe our child *will* want me,' he added harshly.

Bryna paled. 'What on earth are you talking about?' She stood up agitatedly. 'What child?'

His eyes were steely. 'The one you're carrying. My child.'

She regained enough control to be able to give a scornful laugh, although his announcement had badly shaken her. 'I don't know what you're talking about——'

'I called your doctor, Bryna,' Raff interrupted softly. 'He confirmed my suspicions.'

'I don't believe you,' she shook her head. 'A doctor doesn't break a patient's confidence, no matter what the provocation.'

'And I'm sure yours wouldn't have done so this time if he hadn't thought I was already aware of the fact that I'm going to be a father again,' Raff ground out. 'I telephoned him and asked him if he thought your pregnancy was going well; he was only too happy to assure me it was,' he added hardly.

Bryna breathed hard in her agitation. 'What on earth made you call him and ask him such a question in the first place?'

His eyes narrowed. 'You seem to have forgotten

that I've been a father twice before, that I know the signs.'

'What signs?' she challenged.

He shrugged. 'Your extreme tiredness, a sudden aversion to the smell of fish. The fact that——'

'Why didn't you ask me?' A deep blush darkened her cheeks. 'Why call my doctor?'

'I just did ask you,' he rasped. 'You know the answer I got!' he scowled. 'I waited for you to tell me, Bryna, but instead you came up here!'

'Why on earth would you be interested in any pregnancy of mine?' Her agitation deepened.

Raff's eyes narrowed. 'Why wouldn't I?'

Her head went back in challenge. 'Maybe this baby isn't yours!' She didn't care that she was admitting her pregnancy by asking the question; it was useless continuing to deny it when her doctor had already assured him of its existence. It hadn't even occured to her that because Raff had been through two pregnancies with his wife he would know and recognise her own symptoms!

He relaxed slightly. 'I know that it is, Bryna,' he told her quietly.

She gave a pained frown, swallowing hard. 'What do you intend doing about it?'

'What do *you* intend doing about it?' he returned, silkily soft.

'Me?' She gave him a startled look, anger darkening her expression as his meaning became clear. 'How dare you think that I——'

'Bryna!' Her father burst into the room, looking her over anxiously. 'Thank God you're all right!'

She gave him a reassuring smile as she squeezed

his arm, controlling her burning anger towards Raff with effort. 'I'm fine,' she assured him.

'She's just been working too hard,' Raff cut in smoothly, his brows arching slightly as her father gave him a questioning look. 'I'll take her for a walk out in the fresh air.'

'Bryna?'

'Maybe that would be a good idea, Dad.' She gave him a bright smile, her heart skipping a beat as Raff helped her on with her thick anorak before taking his own leather jacket off the back of her father's chair. 'It's a little warm in here,' she excused lightly.

'I'll drive her back to the house afterwards.' Raff's tone dared either of them to dispute his right to do that.

Bryna gave her father's arm another squeeze as he looked at her uncertainly. 'I'll see you lunch-time.'

'He knows, doesn't he,' Raff stated as they walked at the foot of the panoramic mountains, dozens of skiers already on the slopes.

She gave him a brief glance before again watching her footing. 'They both do,' she nodded.

His eyes were steely. 'And yet your mother was polite enough to me when I called at the house, and your father didn't seem too concerned either. I'd want to kill any man who got Kate pregnant when they weren't married!'

'My parents love me too,' she defended resentful-ly. 'They just know I'm mature enough to handle this on my own.'

'You haven't told me how you feel about "this"

yet,' Raff prompted drily. 'Although it's obvious from your reaction earlier, and the fact that you've told your parents, that you don't intend having an abortion.'

'No, I don't,' she snapped. 'Look, Raff, why should I tell you anything?' She stopped to glare at him. 'I meant what I said yesterday; it's over between us.'

His hands moved to tightly grip her arms. 'Our child doesn't think so.'

'Raff, you already have two children, you don't need mine,' she reasoned warily.

'Do you want this child?' He shook her none too gently, his expression fierce.

'Yes!' she shouted at him, tears glistening in her darkened eyes.

'Well, so do I,' he told her softly.

'But why?' She wrenched away from him. 'You can have children with any woman, whereas I——'

'Yes?' he prompted harshly as she broke off abruptly.

She breathed deeply to calm herself. 'This baby is mine——'

'Ours,' he corrected abruptly. 'A sister or a brother for Kate and Paul.'

She had never thought of it from quite that angle before; she had imagined her child looking like the attractive pair, but never thought that her child would have them as a sister and brother.

But as she did realise it she also recognised that *either* of them was old enough to be the parent of her baby. Raff *couldn't* want another baby around him at this stage in his life, just as Kate and Paul wouldn't; he just didn't like to be thwarted.

'That changes nothing,' she dismissed. 'And I wouldn't stop either of them seeing the baby if they wanted to.'

'And what about me?' snapped Raff. 'When would I get to see my child—once a month, two weeks in the summer, and alternate Christmases if I'm lucky?' His disgust with that arrangement was obvious!

'Our lawyers could work something out——'

'They won't "work anything out" because no matter what other plans you may have made you're going to marry me!'

Raff could be arrogant, domineering, even downright unreasonable, but Bryna had never seen him actually lose his temper enough to shout before; his anger was usually cold and controlled. But he was shouting now, and Bryna flinched in surprise. 'Do you really want to start another marriage with a child born only six months after the wedding day?' she reasoned gently.

On one of the warm summer evenings they had spent together in her bed Raff had told her that the reason he and Josey had married so young was because Josey was already pregnant with Paul at the time. They were in love, had taken risks, and they had paid for it with a teenage marriage that could have succeeded despite that, and yet somehow hadn't. She was sure Raff couldn't want a repeat of that.

His mouth twisted. 'It seems I'm destined to get my wives that way,' he derided. 'God, Bryna, there's no comparison!' he dismissed impatiently.

'I'm thirty-nine now, not eighteen. And you are hardly a child either!'

She shook her head slowly. 'I don't want to marry you.'

'Because you no longer want me physically?' His eyes were narrowed to steely slits.

She looked at him unflinchingly. 'That's right.'

A nerve pulsed in his cheek. 'That's easily settled; I won't touch you in a physical way again.'

Bryna looked at him as if he had gone insane right before her eyes, but she could tell by his set expression that he meant every word he said. 'Easily settled'? Could he really stand there and decide in that calm way that he no longer desired her either? It seemed that he could. And wasn't it what she had suspected in their relationship the last month or so? But for the sake of their child he was determined to marry her, no matter what he had to do to get her to agree. And much as her parents loved her and would want to help her, could any of them defy one of the richest men in England, possibly the world? Where could she go that he wouldn't find her!

'I can't give you an answer now, Raff,' she told him tremulously. 'I need time to think.'

He looked pointedly at the flatness of her stomach that would soon swell with his child. 'Time is something we don't have too much of,' he rasped.

Her eyes flashed. 'A few days isn't going to make that much difference!'

'All right,' he gave an abrupt inclination of his head. 'You have a few days.'

And after that he would make the decision for

her, he seemed to be telling her without actually saying the words!

Bryna, of all people, knew how charming Raff could be when he chose to be, and over lunch with her parents he wanted to be very much, talking freely about their life together in London, answering questions about Kate and Paul.

She knew her parents respected the fact that it was her decision what the future held for her and her unborn child, but as Raff solicitously saw to her every need during the meal she could see them both shooting her questioning looks as to why *she* had decided she and Raff were 'no longer together'; it was obvious from Raff's behaviour that it hadn't been his decision to end things! And her parents knew that she loved him, that she would never have become his lover if she hadn't been in love with him from the first.

Their first evening together Raff had deliberately set out to seduce her, with an expensive dinner eaten by candledlight, romantic music playing softly in the background, with a slate-eyed Raff sitting across from her. She hadn't wanted to be seduced, had found his domineering attitude of earlier disquietening, even if she couldn't help but be attracted to him.

She had expected him to take her home by car from the restaurant, instead he had suggested picking his car up later and walking through the park to her home. Her scepticism with this idea turned to enchantment as she realised that no mugger in his right mind would argue with Raff, and that the scent of early summer flowers was even

more heady than the wine they had consumed
during their meal.

The biggest surprise of the evening had come
when he refused her invitation to come into her
apartment for coffee, and instead gave her a
lingering goodnight kiss on her doorstep before
taking his leave. That single kiss had been enough
to tell her she was more attracted to him than to any
other man she had ever known.

When Court telephoned her the next day and
invited her out to dinner with him that evening it
wasn't too difficult to refuse him, knowing she was
keeping her evening free just in case Raff called.
She knew she was behaving like a teenager waiting
for a call from her first boyfriend, but she couldn't
help herself!

He didn't call, and she spent the evening washing
and drying her hair instead, cursing herself for
turning down an invitation from such a nice man as
Court Stevens on the offchance that a rat like Raff
Gallagher might deign to call.

She was still angry with herself the next day, her
mood one of snapping irritation. How could she
have been so gullible as to have been taken in by a
man like Raff Gallagher! He had proved his point,
that they had indeed 'met again', and that like all
the other women in his life she hadn't been able to
resist him!

'Wishing that pencil were my neck?' drawled a
coolly confident voice.

Bryna looked up at Raff Gallagher with a start as
he stood unannounced in the doorway to her office;
she would have a word with Gilly about this

oversight later, *after* she had evicted Raff Gallagher from her office!

'I didn't think you were the violent type,' he raised dark brows as he strolled fully into the room, closing the door softly behind him.

She glanced down at the broken pencil in her hands with some surprise; she hadn't even realised she had snapped it in two. 'I'm not.' She dropped the two halves of the pencil into the bin beside her desk. 'I don't believe we have an appointment, Mr Gallagher.' She looked at him with cool enquiry.

He bent his long length into the chair opposite hers. 'Do you have any coffee? I'm in need of waking up.'

Bryna's eyes flashed angrily. 'Then maybe you should have stayed in bed longer!' How dared he come here demanding she give him coffee after spending the night with one of his women!

He leant his head back in the chair, closing his eyes briefly. 'I haven't been to bed——'

'Mr Gallagher——'

'I must be getting old,' he drawled ruefully, straightening in his chair, just that few seconds' relaxation with his eyes closed seeming to have revived him a little. 'A couple of years ago I would have been able to take flying to the States, working through their evening—our night—and then flying back to England when my business was finished, without any ill-effects.' He shook his head. 'Now I just feel exhausted.'

'Well, of course you do,' scolded Bryna, having listened in horror as he related his gruelling schedule of the last twenty-four hours; no wonder he hadn't called her, he hadn't had time! And she knew how shattering jet-lag could be too. 'You'll kill yourself working that hard!' She stood up to pour him a cup of coffee from the percolator across the room.

He drank the strong black brew gratefully. 'I couldn't give Court the opportunity to move in on the woman I so badly want for myself,' he said softly, watching her over the rim of his cup as he drank some more coffee. 'Now could I?' He looked at her warmly.

A sophisticated lady, used to any amount of male attention during her years as a model, and she blushed! 'Maybe you should have taken the time to telephone me before you left so that I knew you felt that way,' she snapped.

His eyes narrowed. 'Does that mean I'm too late, and Court has called you?'

Was this man ever too late, had any woman ever denied him? Could *she*? 'I think you should go home to bed now, and——'

'Come with me,' he invited huskily, his tiredness completely gone now.

Bryna swallowed hard at the directness of his approach. 'And if you still want to see me again you can call me later,' she finished firmly, resisting with effort the temptation she had to go home with him right now. If he asked again she might not have resisted, but instead he stood up to leave.

'I'll call you later,' he told her throatily.

She faced him across the room; she hadn't returned to her seat behind her desk after pouring him his coffee. 'Fine,' she acknowledged nervously.

Nervous? The woman who had been called icy and distant? Incredible!

'Bryna,' Raff murmured huskily before taking her in his arms and kissing her lingeringly on the mouth. 'I'll definitely call you later,' he told her ruefully as he straightened reluctantly. 'And next time I have to go away on business unexpectedly I'll make sure I call and let you know,' he promised softly.

Next time? Bryna pondered over the statement all afternoon. He seemed to be implying that their relationship was going to be a lengthy rather than short one, and knowing about him what she did she knew that any lengthy relationship she had with Raff Gallagher would have to be a physical one. And before she saw him again she would have to decide if that were what she wanted with him.

If the romantic dinner and the moonlit stroll through the park had come as a surprise to her two days ago when arranged by such a cynical man as Raff Gallagher, then spending the evening at his home with his two children came as even more of one!

Raff had telephoned just before she was due to leave her office for the day, something she was relieved about because she didn't think he knew her home telephone number and so she had been contemplating sitting at her desk waiting for him to call. Even if it took all night!

When he had invited her out to dinner but advised her to dress casually she still hadn't been alarmed. The suspicion had only begun when they turned into the long driveway to his home!

Raff gave a derisive smile at her accusing look. 'I didn't manage to get to bed this afternoon,' he drawled. 'And the thought of sitting in a restaurant and possibly falling asleep in the company of the most beautiful woman I've ever met is not something I relish!'

Her mouth quirked at his self-derision. 'Your reputation would be shot to pieces!' she acknowledged.

He raised dark brows. 'Don't believe everything you hear—or read—about me,' he said drily, opening her car door for her.

She turned from admiring the Georgian-style house situated in Royal Berkshire to smile at him. 'You mean you don't drink champagne for breakfast and wear silk pyjamas?' she mocked one of the articles she had once read about him, although the thought of the latter against the velvet hardness of his skin sent a shiver of pleasure down her spine.

'No,' he grinned.

'No to which one?' Bryna raised blonde brows curiously.

'No, I don't drink champagne for breakfast, and no, I don't wear any sort of pyjamas. But I'm willing to reconsider the first if you'll join me one morning,' he added huskily.

A blush darkened her cheeks. 'Did you say something about dinner . . .?'

'Coward!' he taunted as he clasped her arm lightly in his hand as they entered his home.

The presence in the lounge of the pretty dark-haired girl and a young man as tall and dark as Raff, if not quite as muscular, that he introduced as his children, Paul and Kate, instantly took her aback. She had thought Raff had brought her to his home for the sole purpose of trying to seduce her into his bed, and as she glanced at him she could tell by his expression that he had known exactly what she had thought.

The fact that Kate and Paul obviously intended spending the evening at home with their father, no matter who he had with him, threw Bryna into a state of nervous tension.

'Relax,' Raff advised softly as he sat down beside her on the sofa after handing her the glass of sherry she had asked for. 'My children don't bite!'

They didn't bite, but they were so forthright that they made her more uncomfortable than ever with the bluntness of their questions.

At twenty Paul was very like Raff must have been at that age, and he saw no reason to hide the fact that he found her as attractive as he presumed his father did!

Kate was more interested in discussing fashions with her, and she grabbed on to the subject gratefully. Nevertheless, she felt exhausted by the time Paul left to return to his flat in town and Kate went up to her room to listen to a new cassette she had bought that day.

'What did you think of them?' Raff arched mocking brows as she relaxed for what had to be the first time that evening.

Bryna took her time answering, formulating her opinion now that the pressure was off her. His children—although their ages precluded them actually being that!—were both friendly and without affectation, and it was a reflection on their father, with all the wealth he had at his disposal and the fact that he had been a single parent for the last ten years, that they had turned out as nice and uncomplicated as they were. It was obvious that he loved them very much, and that the protective emotion was more than returned.

But she had found Kate's candour a little unnerving, and Paul had flirted with her endlessly.

Raff gave a brief laugh at her continued silence. 'They don't usually have the effect of leaving people speechless!' he assured her. 'Over the years I've been told that they're brash, rude, inquisitive, and spoilt brats.'

'I don't agree with that,' she instantly protested. 'Kate is just brutally honest, and Paul is—well, he's——'

'I'll talk to him tomorrow about his behaviour towards you tonight,' rasped Raff, his mouth tight.

'Oh no,' she protested again. 'He was only—only——'

'Trying to steal the woman I want.' Raff drew her determinedly into his arms. 'No one, least of all my twenty-year-old son, takes something I want away from me,' he told her arrogantly before his head bent to hers.

Looking at him now, as he chatted amiably with her parents, Bryna couldn't help wondering what she thought she was doing trying to refuse him something he wanted as badly as he seemed to want her child!

CHAPTER FOUR

'YOU'RE very quiet.'

Bryna opened her eyes to look across the luxury of the personalised jet Raff had insisted she join him on during her return flight to London. 'I'm just tired,' she shook her head.

She wasn't just physically tired, but mentally too; she had been fighting a battle with herself all day, talking herself in and out of agreeing to marry Raff as he wanted her to do. She still had no solution to the question he demanded she answer soon.

'Just relax, Bryna,' he rasped. 'No one is going to force you into anything.'

He never had forced her, and she had no doubt that he didn't intend to start now. He had never *needed* to use force with her, just as he hadn't that night they made love after she had remained a virgin for the twenty-four years of her life.

It had seemed strange spending the evening with his children on only their second date, but neither they nor Raff had seemed bothered by the fact, and so she had told herself she didn't care either. Despite her protests that she could get a taxi home, because he had to be feeling exhausted by now, Raff had insisted on driving her home himself.

She turned to him as he parked the car outside her apartment building. 'I won't invite you in because——'

'Invite me in, Bryna,' he urged huskily.

'—you're tired, and——' she broke off as she realised what he had said. 'You want to come in?' She blinked her surprise.

'More than anything,' he nodded, his expression intent.

'But you're tired, and——'

'Bryna, I'm wide awake, and I want you to invite me in!'

What could she say to a forceful request like that? She shrugged her shoulders. 'All right,' she agreed a little dazedly. 'If that's what you want . . .'

'It is,' he said somewhat grimly, following her into the building.

Bryna eyed him warily across the width of the lift as it ascended to her floor, aware that the moment of truth had come quicker than she had thought it would, the evening spent with his children having lulled her into a false sense of security where their own physical relationship was concerned.

Raff was broodingly silent, filled with a tension of his own, and she knew by just looking at him that he would never settle for the basically platonic relationships she had shared with the other men she had dated over the years. As they entered her apartment she knew now was the time to make up her mind what she wanted from him.

'What are you thinking about?'

Raff's harsh voice cut in on her memories, and once again she opened her eyes to look across the width of the plane at him. 'What do you think?' she scorned irritably.

He gave an impatient sigh. 'I thought you were

sleeping until I saw your eyes moving under your lids!' he bit out. 'Why bother to fight it, Bryna; you know you'll have to agree in the end.'

'Is that really the sort of marriage you want?' she flared. 'Two people who don't love each other tied together because of a child they accidentally created! Didn't the failure of your first marriage tell you anything about that sort of arrangement?' she scorned.

'My first marriage didn't fail,' he snapped. 'Josey and I were too young, too idealistic about our feelings, to survive all the pressures we had put on us. But we did respect each other.'

'But it wasn't enough, was it?' Bryna reasoned forcefully.

'This time it will have to be,' he grated. 'You talk as if your pregnancy were my fault,' he snapped. 'We may have created that child, Bryna, but I don't believe it was *my* "accident".'

She felt her cheeks pale. 'I wondered when you would get around to blaming me——'

'I'm not blaming you for anything,' he gave a weary sigh. 'But you did tell me you would take care of birth control. I just presumed that you had.'

As she had presumed nature had done for her years before! She had seen no reason for either of them to use birth control when there was no possibility of her becoming pregnant, although she hadn't chosen to tell Raff that. 'I thought I had,' she told him gruffly, not quite able to meet his gaze.

He shrugged. 'Then you did what you could, and it happened anyway.' He pushed away his seat-belt, crossing the cabin to come down on his haunches in

front of her. 'Bryna, we've been lovers for six
months, we aren't strangers who stumbled into bed
together, with your pregnancy the result of that
night. Would marriage to me really be so terrible?'
he encouraged, gently holding her hands within his
own.

She looked at him searchingly, wishing she could
believe that a marriage of necessity to him wouldn't
be the nightmare she thought it would be. Maybe if
they were strangers it *could* have worked, at least
then she wouldn't hunger for his love the way she
did now. But to live in the same house with him, be
married to him, and know she was only the mother
of his child, would be purgatory! And to be married
to him and have him make love to her out of duty
would be pure hell! She couldn't win whatever she
did, not now that Raff knew about her child.

Her head went back proudly. 'I've already told
you that the only way there would *be* a marriage is if
we led separate lives.'

His expression darkened as he released her hands
to straighten and drop into the seat beside her. 'I
believe *I* said separate beds, Bryna,' he rasped. 'I
have no intention of entering another marriage
where we each have our own sexual partners.'

The colour came and then went in her cheeks.
'That wasn't what I meant at all,' she gasped, the
thought of him leaving her in the evenings to go to
another woman making her feel ill. And yet he was
a sensual man; what else could she expect him to do
in the circumstances? 'I—I suppose I could learn to
live with the fact that you—you have other
women——'

'I couldn't accept your having other men,' he grated. 'If you marry me you'll occupy no one's bed but your own! And if I ever find out you've broken that agreement our marriage will be at an end and I'll do everything in my power to get custody of my child.'

Bryna was very pale, not doubting for a moment that he meant what he said—or his ability to carry it out. It was only because she was so aware of the power he wielded that she was even considering agreeing to his proposal.

His eyes were narrowed grey slits. 'You can carry on working, you can hire a nanny to care for the child, you can do what you damn well please, but you won't give any other man what you deny me!'

He was like a child refusing to let anyone else play with his toy even though he didn't want it himself! Because that was all she would be if she married him, a beautiful ornament for his home.

'Can't you see that it wouldn't work, Raff?' she tried reasoning with him.

'I would make sure that it did work,' he told her arrogantly.

She sighed. 'I'm a person, Raff, with feelings of my own, not some business deal you're putting together!'

'I'm well aware of the fact that you have feelings,' he bit out. 'Which is why I offered you a normal marriage.'

So that she could be a charity case, with Raff making perfunctory love to her so that she didn't need to go to other men! God, she couldn't exist that way. 'The pregnancy is my problem, Raff, why don't you just let me handle it?' she urged forcefully.

'The child,' he harshly emphasised the word, 'is mine. And I want it.'

Again she acknowledged that Raff was never denied anything he wanted badly enough. She was like a caged bird trying to escape the bars, even though those bars were made out of gold. A lot of people would say she was being ridiculous by wanting to escape, but then those people didn't love the man who had the key to the door of the golden cage. Besides, she didn't need his money, she was financially secure herself, although she had nothing like the wealth Raff controlled.

'How do you think Kate and Paul are going to react to this cuckoo in their nest?' she demanded.

His expression darkened. 'This child will be as much mine as they are,' he rasped. 'So they'd better learn to accept it!'

Bryna had run out of arguments for the moment, knowing that the only real one she had was that she loved Raff and he didn't love her. She had no doubts about his ability to be a good and loving father to her child, she knew that with her inexperience in the role he had more reason to doubt her capabilities as a mother!

She closed her eyes. 'All right, Raff,' she sighed, 'I'll marry you. On the condition that I have my own bedroom, and that you never enter it,' she added the last quickly as she saw the blaze of triumph in his eyes, making them appear almost silver.

He nodded calmly, looking nothing at all like a man who had just fought a major battle and won. Maybe because there had never been any doubt in his mind that he would be the victor! 'Agreed,' he bit out. 'But I meant it about there being no other men' he watched her with narrowed eyes. 'If you want to make love then come to me!'

Heat burnt her cheeks. 'That won't be necessary,' she told him coldly. She would rather suffer the agony of unfulfilment for the rest of her life than beg him to make love to her!

Raff's mouth twisted angrily. 'You don't think you'll ever be that desperate, hmm?'

'No!' she snapped defensively, her eyes flashing deeply purple.

He shrugged. 'The offer is there if you want it. We never did get around to drinking champagne together for breakfast,' he taunted. 'But I don't suppose it really matters,' he dismissed, turning away.

It was strange that he should remind her of that night when it had already been so much on her mind today.

The minute her apartment door had closed behind them that night she had known that she wanted him as he so obviously wanted her. And yet her inexperience made her shy, the uncertainty she still harboured about being able to satisfy any man. Physically, outwardly, she was sure she was the same as other women, but Raff was a man who had made love to a lot of women over the years; would he be able to tell that she lacked something inside her that made her into a real woman? There was only one way to find out, she decided, taking a deep breath.

'I've been imagining doing this all evening,' he

groaned as his hands threaded through the softness of her hair to cradle the back of her head as he bent to claim her lips.

That single kiss of the night before hadn't prepared her for the sensual onslaught of the second drugging kiss, Raff's body curved into hers, holding her against him only by his hands entangled in her hair.

Not that she wanted to move away from him, straining against him for closer contact as the pleasure of his touch washed over her in waves, her lips parting beneath the pressure of his, moving together moistly.

Every other thought but Raff and what he was doing to her went out of her head, and she arched her throat as his lips caressed her there with insistent passion, their breaths a ragged rasp in the silence.

'Is it all right for you tonight, Bryna?' he pressed urgently.

She gave him a startled look. 'All right? But——' Colour suffused her cheeks as his meaning became clear to her. 'Yes, I—I'm fine,' she assured him awkwardly.

'Can we spend the night here?' His gaze was intent on her flushed face. 'I would have invited you to stay on at the house with me, but with Kate there ...'

'I understand,' she cut in hastily. God, was this the way it was done—a mutual desire, and they just spent the night together? Probably it was, she was just such a novice when it came to these relationships, and if she hadn't already realised she was falling in love with Raff she wouldn't even be contemplating entering into one of them now. And she didn't want Raff to think she was a complete fool. 'It will be much more convenient if we spend the night here,' she said lightly, throwing her clutch-bag down into a chair, wondering what it had still been doing in her hand in the first place, belatedly realising she could have hit Raff around the head with it as they kissed. Well, from now on she was going to appear a little more sophisticated! 'The bathroom is through there,' she pointed to the rose-coloured door. 'Maybe you would like to use it first,' she invited, congratulating herself on how blasé she sounded as she evasively told him she didn't intend sharing it with him.

'Bryna——'

'I have to remove my make-up and all those other going-to-bed things, anyway,' she added brightly. 'But maybe I should just tell you,' she continued haltingly as he just stood there looking at her. 'That my—experience won't be anywhere near as extensive as your own, and I——'

His hard kiss silenced her. 'I don't want to talk about our pasts or the other lovers we've known,' he said harshly. 'For the moment there's only this,' his kiss was lingeringly thorough. 'We can talk later,' he promised. 'When I don't need you quite as badly as I do now,' he added self-derisively.

Fool! Bryna berated herself agitatedly. Of course he didn't want to discuss the extent of her experience—or lack of it—now. Just as she didn't want to know about the other women he had had in his life. 'Take your time in the bathroom' she

invited abruptly, making a hurried escape to her
bedroom.

God, she hoped Raff didn't realise just *how*
inexperienced she was by her fumbling display of
so-called sophistication!

If he had he certainly didn't show it, sitting back
against the pillows in her three-quarter-size bed
when she emerged from the bathroom after her own
shower, the sheet draped across his thighs revealing
that he was completely naked beneath its flimsy
covering. And she was buttoned up from neck to
ankle in a towelling robe! She also felt like a gauche
teenager without her make-up, while he managed to
look more devastating than ever, less awe-inspiring
with the dark swathe of his hair falling over his
forehead, but just as overwhelmingly attractive.

She suddenly felt more shy than ever, wondering
what she was doing contemplating making love
with this stranger that she believed she was falling
in love with.

And then Raff threw back the sheet to get out of
the bed, magnificent in his golden nakedness, and
Bryna was too bemused by him to notice as he deftly
unbuttoned her robe before letting it fall to the
floor.

Her lack of experience didn't seem to matter as
they kissed and caressed each other; she reacted to
him instinctively, knowing a fierce longing to touch
him in the same way he was touching her.

They made love slowly, tantalisingly, with Bryna
wild for his possession when he finally parted her
thighs to move between them, all thoughts of
inadequacy pushed to the back of her mind as she

felt that brief pain followed by the most wonderful feeling of completion she had ever known, meeting the fierce thrusts of his thighs as he drove them both to, and over, the edge of fulfilment.

Bryna had never felt so free, as if she was completely weightless as she flew on a soft, downy cloud of hazy pleasure.

But as she looked up at Raff as he still lay joined to her some of the happiness faded from her eyes, knowing that for him it had just been another sexual encounter. 'I did try to warn you I'm a bit of a novice at this type of thing.' She couldn't quite meet his gaze, only inches away from her own.

'Novice?' he echoed gruffly. 'It was more than that, you were——'

'Very clever to choose someone as skilful as you for my first lover,' she cut in lightly. 'And admittedly I may not be very experienced, but I'm sure we both know the rules well enough——'

'What rules?' he echoed softly, suddenly still as he looked down at her watchfully.

She smiled, still not quite meeting his gaze. 'No ties, no commitments, we can just enjoy each other!'

'Of course,' he agreed flatly, moving away from her to lie at her side.

Bryna looked at him searchingly. Had she been too hasty, could she have been mistaken about the pleasure he had found from their lovemaking? She was discussing the two of them having an affair, and he hadn't even given any indication that he wanted to see her again!

'Unless tonight was all you wanted——'

'It wasn't,' Raff cut in harshly. 'I have a hunger

for you that won't be satisfied with just one night!'
He kissed her fiercely as he began making love to
her a second time.

And so they had had their affair, but although
their lovemaking always gave her that feeling of
completion, as if Raff were the other half of herself,
it had never been quite as emotionally fulfilling as it
had that first night; the last month or so it hadn't
even made her feel close to Raff any more.

And now she had given up even the little she did
have, to become his wife.

CHAPTER FIVE

CHRISTMAS Eve sounded a romantic day for a wedding, and this wedding had had it all—the breathless bride in her gown of flowing white chiffon and lace, attended by four beautiful bridesmaids, one of them the groom's daughter from his previous marriage, the other three all close friends of the bride, the groom himself looking very handsome and distinguished in his grey morning-suit.

The church had been packed with guests, the bride was given away by her proud father, the vows were exchanged with quiet intensity. The wedding of Bryna Fairchild to Raff Gallagher had lacked nothing.

Unless you looked beneath the fairy-tale veneer and realised the reason the bride was so breathless was because the wedding had all been arranged within a matter of two weeks rather than the months such a lavishly perfect occasion would normally take to organise.

Raff had done all the organising, of course, from insisting she wear a white gown, despite her protest that she really shouldn't, to asking her to choose several other bridesmaids to attend her after she had told him Kate would be enough, to inviting so many guests to the church, and the ballroom of this prestigious hotel for their wedding reception, that after greeting them at the door as they arrived she doubted she would see most of the guests again tonight!

Everyone agreed that it had been a beautiful wedding and now reception, that the bride looked beautiful if a little pale—but then what woman wouldn't have been a little pale when she had just become the wife of that magnificently rich and handsome creature?—she had heard one of her female guests murmur bitchily to her companion.

Raff hadn't been about to deny or confirm the rumours going around during the two weeks before their wedding that the reason for the haste was the expected arrival of the 'third Gallagher heir', as one newspaper had put it. But before too many weeks had passed everyone was going to know that was the reason his bride had looked so pale!

Raff had insisted on telling Kate and Paul about the baby and marriage as soon as they got back from Scotland, and although Bryna hadn't even been able to guess what their reaction would be to either piece of news she was pleasantly surprised by Kate's unreserved pleasure, although Paul seemed to feel slightly embarrassed at the thought of having another sister, or perhaps brother, at his age. But neither of them had openly rejected the baby, which was more than Bryna could have hoped for in the circumstances.

Paul had been his father's best man, of course, with Court waving away Raff's explanations as to why he had chosen his son over him, with the laughing comment that he had already been his best man once and that had been enough, only willing to face the embarrassment of the speech he had had to give after the ceremony once in his life. He had chosen to give Bryna a congratulatory kiss instead.

'Would you care to dance, Mrs Gallagher?'

Hearing herself called that gave her a slight jolt, and her smile was a little shaky as she turned to a teasing Court.

His expression darkened with concern as he saw how strained she looked. 'Maybe you should sit down instead and I'll get you something to eat; you look as if you're about to faint!'

'It's this headdress and veil,' she sighed, easing her scalp where the weight of the diamond tiara held her veil in place. Raff had given her the tiara as part of her wedding present, the matching earrings and necklace being locked away in the family safe for her. The tiara demanded that she have her long hair styled beneath it, but she had insisted that it not be twisted and curled into some style that would just feel tortuous by the end of the day. But the pins that secured the tiara in place dug into her flesh instead.

'Take it off,' Court suggested. 'There's no reason why you shouldn't now. I'll help you,' he smiled, his actions matching his words as he searched for the hidden pins.

'No,' she put a hand up to stop him, looking anxiously about the crowded room in case Raff was watching her. He stood across the room talking with Penny and Janine, two of her bridesmaids, and their partners for the evening. But he was looking straight at her, his eyes cold and condemning. 'Raff wouldn't like it,' she told Court a little desperately.

'Don't be silly,' he frowned down at her. 'Raff isn't the one who's uncomfortable.'

'Please don't worry about it,' she assured him quickly. 'The bride can't walk around without her veil!'

'I don't see why you can't now,' Court dismissed. 'If you——'

'Why don't we have that dance?' and forget about the damned veil! Raff had been determined that *nothing* should go wrong with the wedding, and she knew he included her own behaviour in that.

'But——'

'Don't you want to dance with the bride?' she teased. 'Maybe you're frightened that some of the confetti will give you ideas yourself?' she taunted.

'Not me,' he grinned as he swept her deftly around the dance floor. 'I'm what's known as a "crusty old bachelor"—and determined to stay that way!' he added firmly.

Bryna gave him a scathing glance. 'In that case leave my fourth bridesmaid alone!'

'I happen to find Alyson a very stimulating conversationalist,' he returned in a reproachful voice.

'Of course you do,' Bryna laughed softly. 'That's why you suggested the two of you book into a room here for the night!' She arched mocking brows.

'I was only trying to be helpful by offering an alternative to the journey to her home late at night,' he defended.

Bryna chuckled. 'She only lives half a mile away!'

'That's right, mock my generosity!' Court sounded as if she had offended him, but the twinkle in his eyes belied the emotion. 'Women,' he muttered. 'They can't keep anything to themselves!'

She smiled at him. 'If it's any consolation, Alyson was almost tempted to accept!'

'That's the story of my life,' he bemoaned with a sigh. 'Women are always *almost* tempted.'

'From what Raff has told me about you it isn't always almost!' she reproved.

Court gave a self-satisfied grin. 'We "crusty old bachelors" need companionship occasionally, you know.'

Bryna shook her head. 'No wonder you and Raff are such good friends.'

He sobered. 'Raff hasn't looked at another woman since the two of you started seeing each other. Well—except Rosemary the other week,' he amended awkwardly. 'And that doesn't really count.'

'It doesn't?' she frowned, wondering if he knew something she didn't, because as far as she was concerned that night still smarted very much.

'Well, he should never have let it go that far, of course, but he did have that business deal on his mind, and——'

'Is that what he told you?' she scorned disbelievingly. She had never actually asked Raff what excuse he had given to his friend for his behaviour that night, and Raff hadn't offered to tell her, but now she knew he had told a deliberate lie. Why not just tell the truth, that he was tired of her and looking for a way out?

Over the last two weeks he had consulted her on the finer points of the wedding, overridden her where he didn't agree with her opinion, making her wonder why he had bothered to consult her in the first place. And he had kept to his promise that he wouldn't touch her in a physical way again.

As an example of what their married life was going to be like she learnt just how miserable she was going to be, but as a testament to how well Raff could keep his promise his behaviour had been unimpeachable!

Court frowned. 'You mean it isn't what really happened?'

She looked up at him searchingly. 'Court, Raff did tell you that we're only getting married because of the baby?'

'What baby?' He looked perplexed, his brows disappearing beneath his hair-line at the same time as his gaze lowered disbelievingly to the high-waisted gown she wore, the swelling of the baby barely perceptible beneath its Regency-style lines. 'You're pregnant?' He frowned his disbelief.

Now it was Bryna's turn to look puzzled. 'You mean Raff *didn't* tell you? She had thought that he would at least trust his best friend with their secret.

'You mean you *are* pregnant?' Court stopped dancing to stare down at her, tightly gripping her arms.

'Yes,' she confirmed simply, tears glistening in her eyes.

'There have been rumours, because of the suddenness of the wedding,' he said slowly, still looking dazed. 'But Raff never gave a hint—My God, I never guessed!' His face darkened angrily. 'The stupid——'

'It wasn't Raff's fault,' she cut in quickly. 'I'm afraid I was in charge of that, and I—goofed.'

'And from the look of you he's obviously been making your life hell because of it,' he scowled, scouring the room for the other man. 'How could he do this to you? He——'

'Court, please!' She put a hand of entreaty on his muscle-tensed arm, conscious that they were attracting considerable attention as they stood in the middle of the ballroom while the other couples danced around them. 'Let's go somewhere and talk,' she encouraged. 'I——'

'Stuart has been longing to dance with you, Bryna.' A harsh-faced Raff appeared at her side, his assistant firmly in tow. 'You seem to have concluded your dance with my wife, Court,' he told the other man firmly.

Court looked set to argue that point, but Bryna evaded the scene that would ensue if he did by moving lightly into Stuart Hillier's arms.

As she moved instinctively to the music she was barely conscious of her dancing partner as she watched Raff and Court leave the dance-floor to go into a room together off the main area where all the guests were gathered.

'Your parents seem to be having a good time.' Stuart Hillier's abrupt statement brought her attention back to him, although she couldn't stop feeling anxious about what was transpiring between the two friends behind that closed door.

She glanced across the room to where her mother and father were once again dancing together, returning to the table they shared with Raff's more elderly parents during the short resting periods between dancing. They had always enjoyed dancing together, and as her father had laughingly teased, what better occasion to dance than at their only child's wedding?

Having met Raff, and liked him, they were pleased she had decided to marry him, and she hadn't had the heart to tell them how much this marriage distressed her. They only wanted her to be happy, and they believed Raff could make her that; they could have no idea of the bargain she had made with her new husband.

'Yes,' she turned back to Stuart Hillier. 'I hope you're enjoying yourself too.' She looked at him enquiringly.

'Of course,' he returned stiltedly.

His manner was unfriendly to say the least, and after months of finding him overly familiar, if anything, she couldn't help wondering if he had been warned off by Raff's attitude towards Court a few minutes ago. She hoped so.

She didn't know why she disliked this man, he was always polite, sometimes too much so, and yet for some reason she felt uneasy in his presence. He was reasonably tall, although not as tall as either Raff or Court, with dark hair and deep brown eyes that should have been warm but somehow weren't. He made Bryna feel uncomfortable every time she was with him.

'Good,' she gave him a bright smile as the music ended, turning to walk away, only to have him clasp her arm. 'Yes?' she turned to him enquiringly.

'Raff asked me to—look after you, until he

returns,' Stuart told her challengingly.

'Indeed?' She gave him a look of haughty disdain. 'I don't believe I need "looking after" at my own wedding, thank you!'

'Nevertheless——'

'Mr Hillier,' she cut in icily, 'at this moment I intend talking to one of my cousins, and I certainly don't need your company to do that!'

How dared Raff tell his assistant to watch over her as if she were a child who could step out of line and embarrass him if left alone! He had never acted in that autocratic way with her before, never given the impression she wasn't to be trusted if left on her own. Maybe he expected her to get up on a table and announce to all their guests that they were to be parents in just over six months' time! *That* was going to be obvious soon enough anyway, and she certainly wouldn't embarrass *her* parents by even thinking about doing such a thing!

She was chatting absently with her cousin and her fiancé when she saw Court leave the room he and Raff had entered together, quickly excusing herself to cross the room towards him, a perplexed frown marring her brow as he turned to leave the reception room without a second glance, his expression thunderous.

Bryna hurried after him. 'Court——'

'Don't!'

The pain of having her wrist cruelly grasped was as nothing to the ache in her chest as she looked up into Raff's coldly furious face. He actually looked as if he hated her in that moment! He had never seemed so much a stranger.

She wrenched her gaze away from his cold one, looking towards the door. 'But Court——'

'Had to leave unexpectedly,' Raff bit out in harsh reply.

Bryna turned back to him slowly, frowning her bewilderment. 'You asked your best friend to leave our wedding,' she said disbelievingly.

'No,' Raff grated softly. 'He chose to leave.'

Bryna faced him accusingly. 'Because you made him,' she realised disgustedly. 'What on earth do you think you're doing ——'

'I think I'm trying to avoid causing a scene, but if you're intent on one——!' He nodded in the direction of the room he and Court had so recently vacated. 'Let's go in there,' he instructed between gritted teeth.

Bryna went willingly. She had been woken by her mother at seven o'clock this morning, been hustled and bustled about all morning dealing with all the last-minute details, been married to a man who was now a stranger to her, and for the last four hours she had tried to put a happy face on that marriage in front of their families and friends. It felt good to at last have a respite from that, although she wished it could have been in happier circumstances.

The room turned out to be a small lounge, even a small fire burned in the grate; the room was obviously provided for people who found the festivity in the ballroom a bit much. Bryna wished she had known about it earlier; four hours earlier!

She turned to Raff. 'Why are you being so arrogantly unreasonable?' she demanded.

He looked at her coldly. 'I consider my behaviour

very reasonable,' he snapped. '*You're* the one who insisted on making an exhibition of yourself!'

Her cheeks coloured at the accusation. 'I was only dancing with Court——'

'Forgive me, but when I interrupted you certainly weren't dancing,' rasped Raff, thrusting his long capable hands into his trouser pockets. 'The two of you were drawing attention to yourselves by that mere fact alone, and minutes earlier dozens of our guests witnessed the way he caressed your hair——'

'He wasn't caressing my hair,' she defended heatedly. 'He was trying to take off my veil!'

Grey eyes narrowed. 'Why?'

'Because he's kind.' Tears glistened in her violet-coloured eyes. 'Because the veil was making by head ache!'

'If it makes your head ache why didn't you just remove it yourself?' he challenged.

Because she had known it would displease him! My God, she thought, in the space of just two weeks she had become one of those women she despised, in awe of her husband instead of the independent woman she had always been, fearing his disapproval to the slightest move she made.

She was a successful businesswoman, for goodness' sake, with a mind and will of her own, not some simpering simpleton afraid of her own shadow. Consideration for the feelings of others was one thing, but in Raff's case she had taken it too far!

'I thought I was supposed to keep up appearances,' she told him caustically, deftly removing the pins from her hair, at once feeling the pressure ease.

'But I think four hours is enough for any bride!' She put the tiara and veil down on a small table in front of her, shaking her hair just to feel its freedom. 'Now I intend enjoying what's left of my wedding reception, you can act as watchdog if you want to!' She turned to leave.

'What's that supposed to mean?' he grated harshly, his mouth tight.

Bryna spun around. 'Do you think I'm a fool, Raff?' she scorned. 'I know you've been watching my every move since I agreed to marry you. Why, I have no idea, but I think even you can trust I wouldn't do anything stupid at my own wedding!'

His mouth was taut and unremorseful. 'You've already caused quite a lot of talk by your behaviour earlier with Court——'

'What behaviour?' she demanded impatiently. 'I only danced with him!'

'And told him about the baby,' Raff bit out accusingly.

'He's your best friend, I would have thought you would have already told him!' she retaliated, her eyes blazing deeply purple.

'Why should I have done?' he challenged.

She frowned. 'Because—well, because——'

'It's none of his damned business,' Raff told her coldly.

Bryna gave a weary sigh, her head starting to pound again. 'Look, I don't want anything I've done to be the cause of friction between you and Court——'

'Don't you?' he scorned. 'I thought all women liked men to fight over them.'

Whatever Court had had to say to Raff about her
pregnancy, it had obviously caused a rift between
the two men. 'You and Court have no reason to
argue because of me,' she dismissed impatiently.
'It's ridiculous, and I don't like it——'

'That's just too bad,' her husband snapped.
'Because I have a feeling it's something you're going
to have to get used to!'

'But why?' Bryna reasoned intensely. 'Court is
just upset with you at the moment for not confiding
in him about the baby. He'll come around——'

'But I won't,' Raff warned softly. 'Now we'll
rejoin our guests together,' he instructed coldly. 'I
think it's time they started to leave anyway; you
need to get some rest.'

She was surprised he had noticed how fatigued
she was, only having seemed concerned with
keeping up appearances until now. But maybe that
was it, a new bride should be glowing with vitality
and love for her husband, not just look exhausted!

Luckily some of the guests had decided it was
time for them to depart; if they hadn't she felt sure
Raff would have somehow persuaded them it was
time to go—politely, of course!

Ordinarily, as the bride and groom, they could
have escaped hours ago, but as it was Christmas the
next day they had decided not to go away on a
honeymoon but to spend the holiday period at the
house with their families. As she should have been
spending Christmas with her parents Raff had
invited them to spend Christmas with them instead,
and Raff's parents would be joining them all for the
day too. As honeymoons went it had to be one of the

strangest! Not that she had any wish to be alone anywhere with Raff in the stange mood he had been in since she first agreed to marry him.

It was gone midnight by the time the last of the guests left, Paul taking his girl-friend home before returning to the house later, Kate being driven home by Roger Delaney, a rather pleasant young man she was at college with whom she had decided to invite at the last minute. Raff's parents had chosen to stay at their home in London and drive down to join them for the festivities tomorrow, so that only left Raff, Bryna, and her parents to drive home together.

She awoke as Raff carried her up the long staircase to her room; she must have fallen asleep almost as soon as she got in the car, because she certainly remembered nothing of the journey.

Raff glanced down at her as he sensed she was awake. 'Your parents said to say goodnight,' he told her.

Flatly, uncompromisingly, totally unapproachable. 'You can put me down now.' She twisted in his arms.

His arms tensed as his grip tightened. 'We're almost there now,' he dismissed abruptly.

Despite the fact that they had been married today the gap between them was widening by the minute, and if they were to be even tolerably happy in this marriage it couldn't be allowed to continue. 'Raff, I didn't realise you hadn't told Court about the baby,' she explained regretfully. 'And when I did——'

'You told him anyway.' He pushed open the bedroom door with his foot.

'He's your best friend——'

'And the baby you're carrying is ours, and anything to do with it, *anything* at all, should be decided by us jointly!'

'But—— This is your bedroom,' she realised in alarm; the austere green and cream décor was nothing at all like the warm peach of her own bedroom further down the hallway. She knew exactly what her bedroom should look like, having moved all her things into it yesterday. She was also familiar with Raff's bedroom through the bathroom that connected their two rooms, the housekeeper having given her a detailed tour of the house after she had unpacked. And the room he had brought her to was definitely his!

Raff slowly lowered her to the floor, their bodies moving against each other before Bryna moved abruptly away.

'I'm well aware of whose room this is.' He pulled his tie undone, leaving it dangling about his throat as he unbuttoned the stiff collar of his white shirt. 'It's been a long day, Bryna,' he said wearily. 'Use the bathroom and let's get to bed.' He sat down on the side of the bed to take off his shoes.

The action drew her attention to the king-size bed he had only ever previously occupied alone. None of his women had ever stayed the night in his home. Raff refused to expose his children to that; all their previous nights together had been spent at her apartment.

Bryna moistened suddenly dry lips. 'You said we would have separate rooms——'

'We have separate rooms.' He stood up forcefully to continue undressing.

'But——'

'Bryna, we have guests in the house,' he bit out tautly. 'My son and daughter too. What do you think they'll make of our sleeping apart on our supposed honeymoon?'

She blinked. 'I wouldn't have thought you cared what other people thought.' He never had in the past!

His eyes glittered angrily. 'Your parents believe you wanted this marriage, and when they leave in three days' time I don't want anything we've said or done to have disturbed their peace of mind. My children's feelings are also important to me, but they will also be gone in three days. And until they are we will share this room and this bed if nothing else, at least give an outward impression of normality. If any of them find out the truth later on we can tell them that it's more comfortable for you, and the baby, if you sleep alone,' he added grimly.

Bryna had also dreaded the idea of her parents realising her marriage to Raff had been a matter of compulsion rather than choice. But she now understood Raff's sudden change of mind about Kate moving into Brenda's flat with her; if his daughter stayed here she would realise how estranged her father and Bryna really were.

'Raff, don't make a decision about Kate's future that you'll later regret. I'm sure we can work something out if you——'

'Kate is eighteen, and it's time she realased there's a whole harsh world out there,' he dismissed.

Bryna shook her head, knowing that wasn't the way he really felt. 'You'll regret it if anything happens to her.'

His brows rose. 'What could happen to her?'

She looked down pointedly at her own body. 'I was once a sophisticated innocent, remember?' she reminded him.

His expression darkened and he looked at her coldly. 'Are you saying I'm forcing my daughter out of her home and risking her becoming pregnant?' he rasped.

'No, of course not! I was only—— Oh! She closed her eyes as a wave of dizziness washed over her, and would have fallen if Raff's arms hadn't closed about her. 'I'm sorry,' she shook back her hair, blinking up at him dazedly.

'You're exhausted!' His expression was grim as he sat her down on the bed, turning her slightly away from him to begin undoing the row of pearl buttons down her spine. 'Don't argue,' he warned as she gave a murmur of protest. 'I told you I wouldn't touch you, and I won't. This is just helping an overtired woman, who's eleven weeks pregnant, into bed where she belongs!'

She wanted to protest that she didn't 'belong' in this particular bed, but she didn't have the strength to argue, not when Raff was already slipping the gown from her shoulders. She was too tired to fight him, and sat docilely while he sponged the weariness from her body, returning again and again to the bathroom to moisten the sponge, until he was satisfied that every part of her felt refreshed. She wondered at this thoughtfulness from the man who had been so coldly aloof from her all day, but she was too weary to question it. She didn't even object as he gently sponged the perspiration from the valley between her breasts, although she did murmur a protest as he moved towards her thighs.

'All right.' He straightened, moving to take her nightgown from the chair where he had draped it, a thoughtful maid having laid it out on the bed for her earlier, indication that the staff expected them to share this room tonight too, at least.

Raff dropped the floaty creation of the white nightgown over her head before settling her back on the pillows and pulling the bedclothes up to under her chin as she sighed her comfort.

Bryna had never felt so tired, and she saw Raff's movements through a haze, her lids refusing to obey her command for them to open. But she did know that he removed his own clothes without sparing her a second glance, going through to the adjoining bathroom, the sound of the water being run telling her he intended taking the shower she had longed for.

She fell asleep to the sound of the water falling in the shower.

And she awoke to the caress of Raff's hand on her body.

At first the shought it was a dream; she was too tired to wake up for anything! But her body knew its master, and she returned to consciousness with the sure knowledge that Raff *was* touching her.

She was turned on her side in the bed, but she could feel the warmth of Raff's body inches away from her back and legs, knew he would be completely naked, that he always slept that way. And his arm rested against her hip as one of his hands trailed over her stomach, and lower.

It was exquisite torture to let him continue, and yet it would cause her even more pain to make him stop. But finally it was the former she feared the most, deciding physical discomfort was preferable to the mental anguish if she let him continue.

She moved abruptly away from him, her eyes accustomed to the darkness as she turned to face him. 'Raff, you promised——'

His eyes glittered silver. 'And I kept my promise,' he rasped.

Her eyes widened. 'But——'

'I wasn't touching you, Bryna,' he denied harshly.

'I felt your hands on my body,' she protested, willing herself to be unmoved by the bronze smoothness of his naked chest as he leant up on his elbow beside her, knowing she was failing as her hands longed to touch him, her body still aroused by his caresses.

'I was touching my child,' he bit out harshly. 'We made no agreement about my not doing that!'

Bryna stared at him disbelievingly. It was true, his hand hadn't strayed anywhere but over the slight curving of her body that was his child. But even so——

'Did we?' he demanded forcefully.

No, there had been no mention of him not touching his child; it was her misfortune that she happened to be carrying the child at the moment!

She felt the awakening of sensual pleasure she had known at his touch shrivel and die.

'Get used to the idea, Bryna.' He lay flat against the pillows beside her. 'I intend to be as close to this child as I am to Kate and Paul, and I'll touch it any time I damn well please!' The closing of his eyes and the evenness of his breathing told her that as far as he was concerned the discussion was at an end, whether she chose to dispute his claim or not.

How could she dispute what was, after all, his right?

What father didn't long to touch his unborn child in its mother's womb, to know the wonder of that life before it was born?

The six months left of her pregnancy promised to be a living hell for Bryna.

CHAPTER SIX

CHRISTMAS had always been a time of joy and laughter in Bryna's family, with a visit to church on Christmas morning, a happy closeness as they all prepared the lunch together, sitting around a glowing fire together after they had eaten the sumptuous meal, occasionally dozing in front of its warmth as the food and peace of the day washed over them.

Never having spent Christmas with Raff and his family before, Bryna was a little uncertain about what to expect, although she soon realised that even Raff became caught up in the festivity of the day, the two of them being rudely awakened by an exuberant Kate at only seven o'clock in the morning.

'Time to get up,' she announced cheerfully, wearing her nightgown and robe, looking very young with her face free of make-up and her hair a tumble of glossy black curls.

The transition of shielding their affair from Raff's children to having one of them burst in on them the day after their wedding was a difficult one for Bryna, and she looked awkwardly at Raff as she burrowed under the bedclothes.

Raff looked younger with his hair falling darkly across his forehead, blinking sleepily, a dark growth of beard on the firmness of his chin. 'Shouldn't you have knocked, young——'

'I did,' his daughter told him happily, perched on the end of their bed. 'You didn't answer.'

'Obviously because we were still asleep,' he drawled, moving to sit back against the headboard. 'And if we hadn't been sleeping we *certainly* wouldn't have welcomed the interruption,' he taunted.

Embarrassed colour darkened Kate's cheeks as she stood up. 'Really, Daddy, you shouldn't make too many of those sort of demands on a woman in early pregnancy,' she told him reprovingly.

He scowled as she neatly turned the tables on him. 'How the hell do you know that?'

Kate gave him a derisive look before giving Bryna a conspiratorial smile. 'Maybe now that he's actually going to *have* a baby in the house he'll realise I'm not one any more,' she mocked with a cheeky grin. 'Now do hurry up and come downstairs, Daddy, I want to open my presents.' She abandoned her air of sophistication at the thought of the gifts waiting under the tree for them all, hurrying downstairs to wait for them—and probably to prod and poke about her own parcels until they arrived!

Bryna gave an indulgent smile, feeling closer to Raff than she had for weeks as he returned the smile.

'In one breath she tells me how grown up she is, and in the next moment she looked eight years old again,' he shook his head ruefully.

'We all like to open presents,' she smiled, the fatigue of the night before completely erased after a

NO COST! NO OBLIGATION!
NO PURCHASE NECESSARY!

PLAY "LUCKY 7"
AND GET AS MANY AS SIX FREE GIFTS...

HOW TO PLAY:

1. With a coin, carefully scratch off the three silver boxes at the right. This makes you eligible to receive one or more free books, and possibly other gifts, depending on what is revealed beneath the scratch-off area.

2. You'll receive brand-new Harlequin Presents® novels, never before published. When you return this card, we'll send you the books and gifts you qualify for *absolutely free*!

3. And, a month later, we'll send you 8 additional novels to read and enjoy. If you decide to keep them, you'll pay only $2.24 per book, a savings of 26¢ per book—plus 89¢ postage and handling per shipment.

4. We'll also send you additional free gifts from time to time, as a token of our appreciation.

5. You must be completely satisfied, or you may return a shipment of books and cancel at any time.

FOLDING UMBRELLA FREE

This bright burgundy umbrella is made of durable nylon. It folds to a compact 15" to fit into your bag or briefcase. And it could be YOURS FREE when you play "LUCKY 7."

PLAY "LUCKY 7"

Just scratch off the three silver boxes. Then check below to see which gifts you get.

YES! I have scratched off the silver boxes. Please send me all the gifts for which I qualify. I understand I am under no obligation to purchase any books, as explained on the opposite page.

308 CIP U1B4

NAME

ADDRESS   APT.

CITY   PROVINCE   POSTAL CODE

DETACH AND MAIL CARD TODAY

**Business
Reply Mail**

No Postage Stamp
Necessary if Mailed
in Canada

Postage will be paid by

Harlequin Reader Service ®
P.O. Box 609
Fort Erie, Ontario
L2A 9Z9

DETACH AND MAIL CARD TODAY

good night's sleep. She wished the same could be said of the memory of Raff's hand caressing her body.

'Do we?' he frowned. 'I seem to recall you insisted I *didn't* give you any presents during the last six months,' he added harshly.

'That was because I was your mistress, and not your wife,' she reasoned.

'You weren't my mistress,' he rasped. 'That implies dependency of some kind, and we both continued to live our own lives. We were lovers. And I certainly wouldn't have objected if you had bought *me* presents. In fact, I would have welcomed the knowledge that you thought of me at other times than when we were in bed together.'

The shadow in their depths made her eyes purple. 'Raff, please let's not argue——'

'No,' he grated, shifting in the bed so that he leant over her. 'Happy Christmas, Mrs Gallagher.'

'Happy Christmas,' she barely had time to murmur before his lips merged with hers.

After days of knowing only his cold remoteness she blossomed to the sensual search of his lips like a flower opening to the sun, wrapping her arms about his neck to draw him down to her, returning his passion with a fierce longing of her own.

'Dad, are you—— Don't you know you should treat a woman with extreme gentleness during the early months of pregnancy?' a concerned Paul burst out, his cheeks colouring with a ruddy hue as both Raff and Bryna turned to look at him in surprise. 'Well, you should,' he muttered uncomfortably, wearing a robe over his rumpled pyjamas, his dark hair tousled. 'I read it somewhere,' he added resentfully.

Raff gave a strangled groan as he rolled over on to his back, glowering at his son. 'I was only kissing Bryna, not making love to her,' he bit out irritably. 'What chance do I have of doing that when you and Kate keep bursting in here unannounced?'

Paul shifted uncomfortably. 'I did knock, but——'

'We didn't hear you,' his father acknowledged wearily. 'We are on our honeymoon, Paul.'

'I know, and I'm sorry,' he sighed. 'But if you don't come downstairs soon Kate's going to open everyone's presents!'

Bryna laughed softly once her stepson had gone back downstairs. 'Why do I get the impression that for all their sophistication the rest of the year Kate and Paul become children again at Christmas?' she said drily.

'Probably because they do.' Raff threw back the bedclothes to get out of bed, strolling unselfconsciously across the room to get his dark bathrobe. 'And Paul isn't joking about Kate opening all the presents; one year Josey and I only just got downstairs in time to stop her opening Paul's things; she'd already opened her mother's and mine besides her own! I think we'd better join them now before they come to blows!'

Bryna had seen Raff naked dozens of times the last six months, had even shared in that nakedness, but in the light of their arrangement she felt a little embarrassed about the longing she had to just look and look at him, knowing she was only torturing herself with what could never be.

She turned away abruptly. 'Actually, I think it's a good sign that Paul is taking an interest in the welfare of the baby.'

'You've noticed he's been less than enthusiastic?' Raff sounded troubled.

Bryna gave him a reassuring smile. 'Put yourself in his place, Raff, and see how you feel!'

'Hm,' he grimaced ruefully. 'I suppose it is awkward for him.'

As she watched Kate and Paul dive into their presents under the ten-foot tree that they had all decorated together the previous weekend it was difficult to imagine there would be much of an age gap between her child and them! They were as enthusiastic over the small gifts she and Raff had chosen for them together as they were over the gold watches they also received, and they were obviously truly touched by the thoughtfulness that had gone into the purchase of the books they received from their new grandparents.

Her parents had taken to their new role with gusto, and had already decided that Kate and Paul would be as much their grandchildren as the new baby would be, and Bryna had been delighted to help them choose gifts for both them and Raff, knowing how much he would love the silk tie of pale grey.

She deliberately kept to the background as she watched the rapport between her new family and her parents, relieved beyond words that they were all getting along so well together, giving a start of surprise when Kate dropped a pile of parcels in her lap. She had completely forgotten her own presents.

Her parents had bought her a range of her

favourite perfume, from bath-oil to body lotion, and she smiled at them gratefully. Kate had bought her some books on pregnancy and childbirth, and the two of them shared a smile of understanding. Paul looked a little sheepish about his gift, and she understood why as the rather large box revealed a maternity nightgown.

'Kate helped me pick it out for you,' he put in quickly as his father looked at him with raised brows.

His sister grinned. 'What he means is that he sent me in to buy it and approved it afterwards!' she mocked.

Paul shot her a glowering look. 'Well, I wanted to give her the books, but you insisted that was your gift, and——'

'I love both my presents, thank you.' Bryna kissed them both on the cheek, knowing by the mischievous twinkle in Kate's eyes that she was enjoying teasing her brother about their expected sibling.

'And now mine.' Raff placed a small parcel in the palm of her hand.

She frowned up at him. 'But you've already given me so much, the necklace and——'

'They were wedding presents,' he cut in arrogantly. 'Besides, you bought me a Christmas present,' he reminded her abruptly.

And she knew that he genuinely liked the sculpture she had given him. It was by a relatively unknown English sculptor who they had both agreed would one day be very much in demand. Unfortunately, as with all the greats, it would probably be after his death.

Her fingers shook slightly as she unwrapped the

parcel, the small box revealing an even smaller box inside, and Bryna gasped her stunned delight as she flipped open the lid to reveal a ring. Not an engagement ring, as she had suspected once she saw the size of the box, but a thin gold band topped by seven diamonds. An eternity ring. She looked up at Raff questioningly, but his expression revealed none of his thoughts.

'It's lovely, Daddy!' Kate was the one to enthuse.

It was lovely, and like the wedding band Raff had placed on her finger only yesterday, it was a perfect fit.

Bryna still looked up at him uncertainly, not understanding the significance of the gift. 'It's beautiful, Raff, thank you.'

He nodded abruptly. 'I'm glad you like it. Now I suggest we all get dressed and have some breakfast before my parents arrive and we have to leave for church.'

Because she preferred it, and because she knew her parents felt the same way, Bryna had asked Raff if she and her mother couldn't do the catering for at least Christmas Day, knowing the housekeeper had a sister in Kent she would like to spend the day with. Surprisingly he had agreed to her suggestion, and the cosy family atmosphere increased as the four men talked in the lounge while the four women prepared the meal in laughing camaraderie.

The day passed very much as it would have done at her parents' home, a late lunch of turkey and all the trimmings, *she* being the one to doze off in front of the fire, Raff insisting he and the children would prepare the supper while the rest of them sat down and chatted together. Bryna had been unsure how

Raff's parents would react to the marriage, especially once they knew there was a baby on the way, but they couldn't have been nicer.

Only one thing happened to mar the perfection of the day.

They had finished supper and were clearing away when Kate gave a sudden frown. 'In all the excitement I've only just realised that Uncle Court didn't join us for the day.'

Anger, cold and biting, flickered in Raff's eyes before it was quickly masked. 'He had other commitments,' he shrugged.

Kate wasn't satisfied with that answer. 'But he always spends Christmas Day with us.'

'And after twenty years don't you think he's entitled to a change?' her father demanded.

'But——'

'Kate, we aren't his only friends,' Raff cut in, his tone brooking no further argument.

The subject was dropped, sulkily by Kate, determinedly by Raff, and yet Bryna knew that, in some way she didn't completely understand, she was the one who had caused the friction between the two men that now meant Court no longer even felt welcome in his friend's home.

She felt guilty without really knowing what she had done. It didn't seem possible that Raff could be so angry just because she had told Court about the baby, neither could she accept that it had been because she had danced with Court at the wedding. She had danced with him dozens of times before at parties, and Raff had never objected then. He was behaving unreasonably; she only hoped he soon realised that!

Nevertheless, the incident ruined the rest of the day for her slightly, and she couldn't help wondering if Kate had connected her father's remarriage with Court's absence today, and resented her for it. The girl gave no indication she felt that way, but Bryna couldn't help feeling uncomfortable about the situation. She felt somewhat uplifted by Raff's mother before she left later that night.

'I can't tell you when we've enjoyed a Christmas more.' She kissed Bryna on the cheek; she was a tall woman, as imposing as her son, until you saw her eyes, warm blue eyes that smiled as she talked.

Raff had inherited his grey eyes from his tall and still-handsome father, although in the older man they had mellowed and warmed. 'We had a lovely time, my dear.' He kissed her too.

Michael Gallagher had been a force to be reckoned with himself until his retirement from the business world, and as she watched father and son shake hands Bryna couldn't help thinking what a formidable pair they must have once made.

Raff looked so handsome today, casually dressed in a grey shirt and black fitted trousers, the gold band that perfectly matched her own glinting on his left hand, the watch she had bought him as a wedding gift strapped to his wrist.

Last night she had been too tired to care about their sleeping arrangements, but tonight, despite feeling weary, she was all too aware of them, as she picked up her nightgown to go through to the adjoining bathroom.

No one had guessed at the strain between Raff and herself today, she felt sure, and she knew that was mainly due to Raff and the way he had cared for her in a way that didn't smother her. Was it only because he was concerned about the health of his child, or did he genuinely care about her welfare? The answer to that question was all too obvious—and painful.

She had turned on her side and was pretending to be asleep when he came back from the bathroom and climbed into bed beside her, turning to face her as he had the previous night, his hand moving to rest possessively on the baby.

The heat began between her thighs and radiated outwards, the warm ache making her tremble.

'Are you cold?' Raff questioned gruffly.

Cold—she was on fire! The trembling increased, her breathing becoming ragged, the instructions her brain passed to her body to calm down were completely ignored. How *could* she calm down when she wanted him so much!

'Do you want me, Bryna?' he huskily voiced her pained longing.

To say yes would be to completely abandon her pride, to accept the charitable lovemaking he offered. And she couldn't do that.

'I'm sure you're perfectly well aware from your first wife's pregnancies that women often feel highly—emotional during pregnancy,' she dismissed curtly, remaining rigidly turned away from him.

'Highly sexed, you mean,' he amended bluntly. 'I told you, Bryna, you only have to ask.'

She closed her eyes in pain, gritting her teeth in an effort to resist the impulse she had to turn into his arms and *plead* for his lovemaking. 'I'm really not in the mood, Raff,' she lied, the ache as intense as ever. 'Did you ask Court not to come here today?' she abruptly changed the subject, hoping talking about Court would help her forget the ache.

The hand that had been moving rhythmically across her stomach stopped for a moment, before continuing more determinedly. 'No, it was his own decision,' Raff returned harshly.

'Because of yesterday?'

'Among other things,' he bit out.

'What other things?' she queried tensely, blinking in the darkness.

'I don't want to talk about this just now.' His hand was removed as he turned to lie on his back.

With that intoxicating hand removed she felt able to turn and face him. Raff was making no effort to go to sleep, his eyes clearly open as he stared up at the ceiling. 'It's important to me, Raff,' she began.

'I know that,' he scorned, his eyes glittering dangerously in the darkness.

Bryna's cheeks were flushed. 'Kate and Paul will resent me if they think I had anything to do with your argument with Court,' she snapped.

His mouth twisted. 'I'm sure Kate's and Paul's opinion is very important to you.' he sneered.

'Of course it is,' she defended heatedly. 'Also I don't like to be the cause of a rift between you and Court when there's no reason to be.'

'No reason?' Raff loomed up out of the darkness as he moved to a sitting position, anger in every taut line of his body, the politeness of the day obviously over. 'You flaunted your affair with Court at *our* wedding and you simply expected me to accept it

without retaliation?' He sounded incredulous—and
furious.

The ringing in her ears made her head spin.
Affair with Court—? Raff couldn't be serious!

But as he viciously flicked the switch on the
bedside lamp, the cold fury in his face unmistakable, she knew that he was perfectly serious. But
why? She had never given him cause to think such a
thing

'Raff, how could I have been having an affair
with Court when I was already having an affair
with you?' she reasoned in bewilderment.

His mouth thinned. 'I admit, being unfaithful to a
lover is a little unique?'

'And untrue,' she claimed incredulously. 'What
on earth made you think such a thing? I——'

'I didn't just *think* it, Bryna,' he rasped. 'I have
proof.'

She became suddenly still, wondering if she could
possibly have fallen asleep without realising it and
this was all a nightmare. But as she pinched herself
and felt the pain she knew she was wide awake, that
this was all very real. 'What proof?' she asked
dazedly.

'You were seen having lunches together, cosy
little dinners for two——'

'I told you about them,' she defended.

'Not all of them,' he grated.

'Most of them.' Guilty colour darkened her
cheeks. Her decision not to discuss her business
with Raff in an effort to make him realise how he
shut her out was backfiring in a way she could never
have envisaged! 'They were business meetings.'

'Your contract with Court ended weeks ago,' Raff dismissed coldly.

'I was trying to interest him in using several of my models again,' she told him heatedly.

'Of course you were,' Raff said with obvious scepticism.

'But I was! I—have you spoken to Court about any of this?' she asked exasperatedly.

'Of course,' he nodded abruptly. 'He denies that the two of you are having an affair.'

'There you are——'

'But of course he would,' Raff insisted unrelentingly. 'But you're married to me now, expecting my child, and I don't have to pretend ignorance any more.'

'If you really believe that we had an affair behind your back how do you know this isn't his child?' Bryna challenged, hurt and confused by the unexpectedness of his attack.

'That's the one thing I can be sure of.' He looked at her coldly as he climbed out of the bed. 'You see, Court is sterile!'

Bryna knew she must have paled, but the irony of Court's tragedy after years of believing herself incapable of ever having a child made it too unbearable to contemplate his torment.

But it didn't diminish the fact that as far as Raff was concerned the only thing he could be sure of was the paternity of her child!

It also explained his threats to force her into marriage with him. Maybe he had thought, knowing of Court's sterility, that the other man would be more than glad to marry her himself once he knew she carried a child. She realised now that it was probably also the reason he hadn't told Court about the baby.

Oh, now she understood what he had meant that day in Scotland when he had told her he 'didn't care what other plans she had made, she was marrying him'! He couldn't take the risk that Court would welcome her pregnancy with open arms.

My God, she thought, was the affair he believed her to have been having with Court the reason he had been acting so coldly towards her the last couple of months, the reason he had been so unreasonable and hurt her by flirting with Rosemary the night of Court's party, before making love to her so exquisitely?

If that were so, did it also mean that he hadn't tired of her at all but had believed she was being unfaithful to him?

She looked at him with wide eyes as that last thought occurred to her, realising for the first time that he was in the process of dressing, black trousers already fitted to his narrow hips and legs, a cream shirt unbuttoned down his chest. 'Where are you going?' she asked in dismay; he couldn't walk out on her now, not without discussing this further!

'Out,' he rasped.

'But——'

'Don't worry, Bryna, I'll be back before morning,' he bit out derisively. 'And I'll think of a good excuse for you to move back into your own bedroom tomorrow night!'

'Raff, we have to talk——'

'It's too late for that,' he grated, thrusting his shirt into the waist of his trousers. 'It was too late the moment you decided to take Court as your next lover!'

'But I didn't——'

'Was he as experienced as me, Bryna?' he demanded coldly. 'As "skilled"? Of course he was,' he answered disgustedly. 'But no other man, not even one I once called friend, is going to bring up a child that I know is mine!'

'Raff!' Bryna cried out as he reached the door. 'Raff, it isn't true,' she pleaded. 'None of it's true!'

'I told you, you were seen together,' he rasped contemptuously. 'And even if you hadn't been, do you think I can't tell when a woman changes towards me in bed? My God, I've had one wife who preferred another man to me, so I should know!' he scorned.

She drew in a ragged breath. 'If I did change it was only because——'

'Yes?' he prompted harshly.

'Because *you* changed,' she accused, standing up agitatedly. 'Oh yes, you did,' she insisted at his sceptical expression. 'I thought you were getting tired of me. I thought——'

'You would line up another lover for when our affair was over,' he finished disgustedly. 'What's the matter, Bryna, now that you've discovered the "joys of sex" can't you do without it for even the length of time it would have taken you to find my replacement once our affair was over?'

'Stop twisting things to suit your own warped accusations,' she cried. 'You've got it all wrong,' she insisted emotionally. 'Court isn't, and never will be, my lover!'

'The past I can't do anything about, but you're

right about the future,' Raff told her grimly. 'No
other man is going to know your body but me in
future. And now that I know how much you like to
make love I don't expect I'll have to wait long
before you come begging me to take you!'

Bryna stared at the door he had closed forcefully
behind him without actually slamming it and
waking up the rest of the household.

Did he really believe all that he had accused her
of? Of course he did, he wouldn't be acting this way
if he didn't!

Court and her? How could he have come to such
an erroneous conclusion? She and Court were
friends, yes, and Court flirted with her endlessly,
but surely no more than he did with every other
female he came into contact with.

Proof, Raff had said, but surely he couldn't count
a few meals together where they discussed business
as that? He did, she knew he did, and it seemed
there was nothing she could say to change his mind.

No wonder his cold indifference had actually
seemed to turn to hate since he had found out about
the baby and he had forced her into marriage!

Only now he was making no secret of that hate—
or the reason for it.

CHAPTER SEVEN

BRYNA was glad when the holiday period was over and she could get back to work, away from the oppression of living with Raff.

As promised, he had let her move back into her own bedroom, but he had arrogantly offered no explanation to anyone who might be curious about this abrupt estrangement between husband and wife.

Her parents had gone back to Scotland, Paul had returned to his flat, and she had helped Kate move in with Brenda, still having misgivings about the advisability of the latter. But Raff made it obvious he didn't wish to discuss his daughter, or anything else, with her.

They were living like complete strangers only ten days after their wedding, not bothering to make polite conversation even over dinner now. In fact, the strain at the dinner table had been so intense that the last two evenings Bryna had asked for a tray in her bedroom. As far as she was aware Raff hadn't even noticed her absence!

'Get me Mr Stevens on the telephone, Gilly,' she requested as soon as she walked into her office on her first day back at work.

She leafed listlessly through the mail Gilly had left on the desk for her attention as she waited for the call to come through. She had been longing to speak to Court, to see what he made of Raff's ridiculous accusations, ever since Raff had hurled them at her, but she knew that if she had called him from the house and Raff found out about it—! Well, there was enough friction between them already.

She snatched up the receiver as soon as the telephone rang. 'Court?' she said breathlessly.

'Bryna?' He sounded surprised to hear from her.

Which wasn't surprising if Raff had launched the same accusations at him that he had at her! 'Court, we have to talk,' she told him without prevarication.

'My God, he didn't upset you with his fantasies in your condition, did he?' he returned disgustedly.

'I can't seem to convince him they are fantasies,' she confirmed shakily, feeling like crying after the last days of tension.

'Bryna, he—he hasn't hurt you, has he?' Court demanded concernedly.

'No, of course not,' she protested the suggestion. Raff was a very physical man, who could display displeasure as easily as he could give pleasure, but she was sure he would never use violence on a woman. 'I just need to talk to someone who understands how I feel.'

'Thank God for that,' said Court with obvious relief. 'Okay, Bryna, how about lunch?'

They made the arrangement to meet at the restaurant before Bryna rang off to get caught up in the rush of the day; she had plenty to do after the long Christmas and New Year break. She was glad of the hectic pace of the morning, she had felt as if her life had plummeted completely out of control since the night Raff had accused her of having an affair with Court. With any luck she could continue to work until the day the baby was born!

Court gave her a searching look when she joined him at their table. 'I know you're supposed to tell a pregnant woman how radiant she looks, but you don't look at all well, Bryna,' he frowned as they both sat down.

She knew the truth of that; she rarely slept and had a complete lack of appetite, knowing that both things showed in her lacklustre hair and shadowed eyes. Her pregnancy was becoming very noticeable as she lost weight and the baby inside her grew, the loose dress she wore doing little to hide that fact.

'It's Raff and this stupid idea he has that we had an affair,' she sighed, shaking her head when the waiter enquired if she would like a drink, her fingers moving nervously against the tablecloth.

'When did he tell you about that?' All the laughter had been erased from Court's face and eyes, his own strain very evident.

She shrugged. 'When we got to bed after spending Christmas Day with our families. He——'

'Trust Raff to at least take his damned wedding night before alienating you!' he said disgustedly.

'But he didn't! I mean, we didn't,' she amended with a blush. 'We have this agreement, you see——'

'What sort of an agreement can a newly married couple have that involves them not making love on their wedding night?' Court looked dumbfounded.

Bryna signed. 'The sort of agreement where the father wants complete rights to his as yet unborn child.'

'And that's the only reason he married you?' Court realised incredulously.

Her gaze lowered to the snowy white tablecloth, absently realising that she had badly creased the crisp linen with the constant pleatings of her restless fingers. 'The only reason,' she confirmed huskily.

Court leant back in his chair with an angry sigh. 'You would have been better off fighting him for custody in court!'

'I think that's the reason Raff married me so quickly and then didn't tell me what he believed about the two of us until I was safely his wife,' she told him dully.

'The damned fool,' said Court angrily. 'Why on earth is he throwing your relationship away?'

Bryna shook her head. 'He says he has proof, that the two of us were seen dining together.'

'Business meetings,' he claimed instantly.

'I told him that, but——'

'He didn't believe you,' Court bit out. 'Telling me about his suspicions at the wedding was one thing, but I had no idea he was going to make you unhappy with them too. I would have come to the house even though I wasn't welcome, if I'd known.'

Her mouth twisted ruefully. 'He would have thrown you out, literally. But Kate asked after you——'

'I've seen her,' he nodded grimly.

'You have?' Bryna looked at him in surprise; Kate had come home for dinner three nights ago— the last time Bryna had eaten with Raff—and she had given no indication that she had seen her Uncle Court.

He shrugged. 'She telephoned me and we had dinner together last night. Don't look so worried, Bryna,' he drawled. 'Raff may not want to know me any more, but I've known those kids so long that sometimes I feel as if they're mine!'

Knowing what she did about him she could understand how he felt about the children of his best friend. 'They're very fond of you too,' she nodded.

He gave an indulgent smile. 'Kate is enjoying sharing a flat.'

'Raff doesn't approve,' Bryna frowned. 'He only agreed to let her go so that she shouldn't realise we were living in the same house but apart.'

'The fool!' rasped Court. 'What the hell is the matter with him?' he added angrily.

'I don't know,' she said shakily. 'It all seems to come back to the fact that for some reason he believes the two of us are having an affair.'

'If I didn't know better I would say he was jealous,' Court frowned.

'Impossible!' Bryna gave a scathing laugh. 'If it weren't for the baby I would be out of his life and forgotten by now!'

'Hm,' murmured Court. 'It was because of Kate and Paul that he and Josey stayed together as long as they did.'

'Yes,' she acknowledged dully. 'Now he intends for us to have the same unemotional marriage.'

'It doesn't sound to me as if he wants you to take a lover,' Court derided.

She looked at him searchingly. 'You know about the relationship he and Josey had?'

'That they both had lovers?' he nodded. 'I think everyone knew except Kate and Paul. I can't believe that Raff would settle for that half-marriage again.'

'It isn't a question of settling for anything,' she told him heavily. 'He wants his child. And so do I!'

Court looked at her closely. 'You love him, don't you? Of course you do,' he said self-derisively. 'Why else would you have married him?' His hand covered hers comfortingly.

Bryna shook her head. 'Believe me, Court, if I had any choice I would never have become his wife. But he more or less threatened to take my child away from me if I didn't agree.'

'You——'

'Hello, darling,' greeted a smoothly controlled voice, and Bryna's stricken gaze raised to meet the coldly furious one of her husband. 'I told you I would try to get here, didn't I?' he added lightly.

Bryna knew that the last was added for their audience, that he didn't want anyone to realise his wife was having lunch with another man without his knowledge.

Oh God, she thought, how much of her conversation with Court had Raff overheard! Certainly the part about her having no choice but to marry him, if the angry glitter of his eyes was anything to go by, but he didn't look as if he had also heard Court claim she was in love with him, Raff.

Court sat back in his chair as he released her hand, relaxed and in control. 'Why don't you join us?' he invited politely.

'Unfortunately I'm with some business associa-

tes,' Raff bit out. 'Otherwise, believe me, nothing
else would give me greater pleasure than to join the
two of you and listen to some more of this
fascinating conversation!'

Bryna swallowed hard. He *had* overheard the
part of the conversation where she had expressed
regret at having to marry him. And he didn't look in
the mood to be convinced that it was the *having* to
marry him that bothered her, not actually having
him as her husband.

'Don't cause a scene, Raff——'

'Believe me, I'm very much in control,' he glared
at the other man. 'If I wanted to cause a scene I
would have punched you in the face and taken back
my wife as soon as I came into the restaurant and
saw the two of you together!'

Court's mouth twisted derisively. 'I thought I was
supposed to be the one with the temper?'

Raff looked at him coldly. 'We all know that's my
child Bryna is carrying,' he rasped. 'And I've
warned her what will happen if she sees you again!'

She paled at the veiled threat. 'It's only lunch,
Raff——'

'My wife of ten days lunching with my supposed
best friend!' he scorned, his hands clenched at his
sides, although for their audience his expression
remained pleasant enough. 'Most people would say
the honeymoon bed hadn't had time to cool!'

'The way I heard it it didn't even get lukewarm!'
Court challenged, his own anger evident now, then
he turned to give Bryna an apologetic look as she
gasped. 'I'm sorry, Bryna, but——'

'That can easily be remedied,' Raff bit out

between clenched teeth. 'Starting tonight!'

'Raff, you can't mean that!' She looked up at him with haunted eyes, sure that to have him make love to her out of anger would be worse than the charity she had been imagining it would be.

'Oh, can't I?' he challenged, looking at her with disgust. 'Why don't we wait and see what I can or can't do!'

Bryna watched him as he strode across the restaurant to rejoin the people he had obviously arrived with, three men she didn't recognise, and Stuart Hillier; she wondered what they had all made of his abrupt departure seconds ago.

'I can't believe it,' Court said dazedly. 'I've never seen him like this before.'

She had never seen *anyone* as angry as Raff had been a few minutes ago. It had been worse than the night nine days ago, worse than all the days since; he had been totally out of control.

'I thought you said he wasn't violent.' Court looked troubled.

'He isn't—he hasn't been,' she amended, knowing that was no longer true. 'Oh, Court, what am I going to do?' she cried.

'Don't go back.' He clasped her hands. 'I have a spare bedroom at my flat. We could——'

'I couldn't stay with you,' she shook her head. 'The mood Raff is in, he would kill us both!'

He frowned darkly. 'Which is exactly why I don't think you should go back to him!'

She shook her head. 'He wouldn't hurt me,' she claimed shakily.

'That wasn't the impression I got just now,' Court said drily.

Or her! Raff had looked as if he would like to crush her with his bare hands! 'He'll have got over his anger by the time he comes home,' she said with more confidence than she felt. 'And then we'll be able to talk.'

Court still looked worried. 'If you're sure you'll be all right . . .?'

'Of course I will,' she dismissed lightly, all the time conscious of the man across the restaurant as he pointedly ignored her and Court in preference of charming his dining companions. And she didn't doubt that he was aware of her every move! 'I don't think I'll bother with lunch after all——'

'You and the baby have to eat,' Court told her firmly. 'Just ignore him, as he's ignoring you.' He signalled the waiter to come and take their order.

It was hard to ignore someone when their disapproving vibrations could be felt across the crowded room, but somehow Bryna managed to eat a small amount of the meal under Court's indulgent coaxing. The five men were still sitting at their table when she and Court stood up to leave a short time later, and she deliberately kept her face averted, although she sensed Court's movement as he gave a terse inclination of his head in parting.

She was trembling once they got outside. 'I'm so sorry you've had to be involved in this ridiculous situation,' she told Court shakily. 'I just can't seem to make Raff see sense.'

'Hm,' he looked thoughtful. 'I still wouldn't rule out jealousy. You know, he——'

'I would,' she scorned firmly. 'Jealous men don't look at a woman with hate in their eyes!'

'Maybe not,' he acknowledged slowly. 'But if he feels nothing for you why does he still doubt you when you claim our meetings have all been because of business?' he reasoned.

'Because I didn't tell him about them at the time,' she sighed. 'I hadn't been discussing my business with him for some time. You see, he always shut me out when it came to his business affairs, and so I thought if I stopped telling him about mine he would realise how shut out he makes *me* feel, and then perhaps open up to me a little,' she explained with a grimace.

'Oh, my God.' Court closed his eyes. 'I recognise my own advice there!' He looked at her apologetically.

'Yes,' she acknowledged ruefully. She and this man had become good friends during her relationship with Raff, and she had often confided in him, realising that he knew Raff much better than she did, than she ever would.

'I'll learn to keep my opinions to myself in future,' he groaned.

She squeezed his arm reassuringly. 'It was very sound advice,' she consoled him. 'Unfortunately, I think the man in question has to be in love with you and sensitive to your feelings for it to work!'

Court gave a grimace of regret. 'If you need someone to talk to again, just call me.'

Bryna had a feeling that was going to come sooner than she wished!

Raff didn't come home for dinner, and he didn't

telephone to say he would be late either, leaving her to wonder where he was and who he was with—and some of her conclusions were upsetting, to say the least.

She kept remembering how angry he had been to see her with Court earlier, remembered clearly the reckless glint in his silver eyes. And she knew he was with another woman. Probably the willing— and waiting!—Rosemary Chater.

The looks the other woman had shot at her during the wedding had been positively venomous. How she must be gloating now!

Bryna spent the evening alternating between anger and despair, waiting downstairs in the lounge for Raff to come home.

When he hadn't arrived shortly after eleven she decided she might as well go to bed; it didn't look as if he were coming home at all tonight!

She had only been in her room a couple of minutes when she heard the front door open and then slam shut, the sound of running feet on the stairs. Indignation and apprehension shone in her eyes as she turned to the door as it was flung open, her dress gaping at the front where she had just unbuttoned it.

There was a dark flush to Raff's cheeks as he slowly closed the door, the reckless glitter still evident in his eyes. 'Ah good, I'm just in time for the floor-show,' he bit out contemptuously, leaning back against the door to watch her with narrowed eyes, his arms folded across his chest.

Bryna pulled the edges of her unbuttoned dress

together. 'If you want to see a show go to a strip-
tease club!' she snapped.

He shook his head. 'The thought of watching
some woman I don't know throw off her clothes in
front of a room full of people does nothing for me!
Where did you spend the afternoon?' he suddenly
rasped in a lightning change of mood.

She blinked at the attack. 'At my office,' she
replied grudgingly; what right did he have to
question her?—he was the one who had been
missing all evening!

'I called there several times, but you weren't
there,' he grated accusingly.

Her head went back in challenge. 'I was
unavailable, that's hardly the same thing.' She had
known of each of his calls and had told Gilly to tell
him she was too busy to talk to him. Gilly had
looked at her strangely at the request, but Bryna had
offered no explanations for her behaviour. If she
had even tried she would probably have broken
down and cried. And once she started she wouldn't
be able to stop.

She had no intention of breaking down; she
intended going on with her life with or without
Raff's love. She had survived the trauma of
believing herself infertile, and now that she carried
Raff's child she could surely survive not being loved
in return by him.

But not if he continued to treat her with
contempt, and demanded his rights in her bed!

'Unavailable to me only, I'm sure,' he bit out,
moving away from the door to come towards her,
the intent in his eyes unmistakable. 'You couldn't

wait to get to your lover to tell him what a fiasco our marriage is, could you?' he grated.

'That isn't the way it happened,' she gasped protestingly. 'I met Court——'

'To discuss business?' Raff quoted the past excuses she had given him.

Colour darkened her cheeks. 'No. Not this time,' she added quickly as his eyes glittered silver. 'But in the past, yes,' she insisted firmly. 'Today I—I just needed someone to talk to!'

'And what better choice than your lover?' he taunted. 'What a pity neither he nor your secretary are here to tell me you're unavailable now!'

Bryna didn't fear his lovemaking, she knew that he could never hurt a woman in that way, but what she did fear was that she would respond to him— and that he would know she did!

She picked up her nightgown. 'A bathroom door will do as well,' she told him at the same time as she opened the door and then closed and locked it behind her, hastily moving to lock the other doors before leaning back against the wall, trembling in her apprehension, well aware that if he wanted to he could break the flimsy locks on any of the doors with one forceful kick.

Complete silence followed her escape, and she moved to the door, listening intently.

'We have all the nights of the rest of our lives, Bryna,' Raff murmured suddenly against the closed door.

He made it sound like a prison sentence!

CHAPTER EIGHT

DESPITE his threat, and her fear of it, Raff seemed to avoid Bryna more than ever during the next few weeks, always having left for the office before she got down in the mornings, rarely coming home for dinner, and when he did he asked for a tray in his study. The only time they had actually spent together had been her visit to the obstetrician.

Raff was adamant that he be involved in all aspects of her pregnancy, asking the doctor more questions than she did, some of them making her blush.

When she was sixteen weeks along in her pregnancy he insisted on coming along to the hospital with her while she had her scan, and the two of them watched in fascination as they saw the movements of their baby in her womb, every tiny part of it looking perfectly formed.

After they had shared such a moving experience the antagonism between them seemed completely unworthy of the occasion.

'I watched your face earlier,' Raff spoke gruffly on the drive home. 'You want this child very much, don't you?'

Some of her happy glow evaporated as she gave him a sharp look. 'Of course I do!'

'There's no need to be on the defensive,' he sighed. 'I wasn't being nasty.'

Bryna turned to stare out of the window beside
her, blinking back the tears. She had been plagued
with none of the morning sickness that such a lot of
women complained of, she felt in extremely good
health, but she was so emotional that she cried at
the slightest thing; a sad programme on the
television, a beautiful love story, watching small
children with their parents in the park.

'As you looked at our baby your face glowed with
pride,' Raff told her huskily.

'It's a miracle,' she told him with more feeling
than he could ever understand. If they had been
closer perhaps she would have been able to tell him
of that operation in her youth and the years of
emptiness afterwards, and he would have understood the wonder she felt at actually seeing the tiny
baby inside her body. But they were further apart
now than they had ever been.

'Bryna, is it too late for us?'

She turned to him frowningly, seeing the regret in
his eyes before his attention returned to the road in
front of them. 'What do you mean?' she asked
suspiciously.

'We're married, in another twenty-four weeks
we'll have a child of our own; don't you think we
should try to make this marriage work?' he
prompted huskily.

She wanted nothing else but for their marriage to
work, but she didn't see how that was possible when
he believed she was having an affair with another
man. 'And Court?' she probed frowningly.

His mouth tightened. 'I can't change the way I
feel about you and him, but I realise you're making

an effort, that you haven't seen him since that day
in the restaurant.'

She hadn't; she had felt it best not to aggravate
the situation any further—but how did Raff know
that? 'You've spoken to Court?' she said eagerly,
willing the two men to be friends again.

'No,' he rasped harshly.

'Then how did you—Raff, no!' she cried as she
shook her head, feeling suddenly sick. 'You haven't
had me followed?'

His head went back arrogantly. 'How else was I
supposed to find out what my wife has been doing
with her life lately?'

'You could have asked me,' she groaned, hating
the thought of some faceless person following her
every movement. 'I hope he's entitled to boredom
money,' she added disgustedly. 'Because watching a
woman leave home for work, and then seeing her
come home again and staying in for the evening,
must be the most boring assignment he's ever had!'

'Bryna——'

'Don't touch me,' she avoided his hand as he
reached out for her. 'Just take me back to my office,
I have some work to do.'

He frowned. 'It's after five——'

'So I'll take a leaf out of my husband's book and
"work late",' she snapped tauntingly, sure that
working was the last thing he did on those evenings
he arrived home late, even though Raff did always
telephone now and give that excuse. 'I hope you've
warned your latest lover that you're having her
followed!' She and Court had been 'seen', he had

said; he hadn't told her it was by a professional snooper!

'I don't have a lover,' he bit out grimly. 'And I've only had you watched since that day at the restaurant.'

'Why?' she groaned. 'Couldn't you trust me? Couldn't you——'

'Bryna, as soon as you got back to work you ran to him,' Raff grated. 'What was I supposed to think?'

She shook her head sadly. 'I don't think you've been doing much of that at all lately!'

He breathed raggedly. 'Bryna, I've been through one marriage where my wife took a lover——'

'You told me you both had lovers,' she protested the accusation.

'At first we did,' he conceded. 'And then I became sick of the lies—to the women involved, not to Josey. Oh, I still went to bed with a woman when I felt the need, but it was always only the one time, and always with a woman who expected nothing else from me. Josey's answer was somewhat different,' he added grimly. 'She found herself one lover and stayed with him, all the time refusing anything permanent with him because of the children.'

'How unhappy you must both have been,' Bryna sighed at the waste of it all.

He nodded. 'Which is why I don't want it to happen again with you. We were happy together once, Bryna, we could be again,' he added encouragingly.

'With you having me followed and personally avoiding me every chance you get!' she scorned.

'I've been working late because I had no reason to come home,' Raff told her quietly. 'But we could start again, tonight——'

'And your "employee"?' she bit out tautly.

He sighed. 'I'll get rid of him. Bryna,' he clasped her hand with his as it rested on her thigh, 'let's try!'

She was tempted, oh, so tempted; she still loved him in spite of the bitterness of their marriage. And maybe if they could become close she could convince him that there never had been anything between Court and herself. It still distressed her that she was the cause of the rift in the friendship.

'I'd like to——'

'Then let's do it!' he encouraged firmly.

She looked at him searchingly. 'And what happens the next time I have to see Court? I do want to do further business with him, you know.'

Raff's jaw clenched. 'I suppose I'll just have to learn to live with that. As long as you can assure me nothing is going on between you except business I'll believe you.'

'You haven't believed me so far,' Bryna reminded him wearily, wondering if this sort of truce between them could really work, but like him, doubting their marriage could survive as it was for much longer.

'My trust has taken a pounding the last few months, that's all,' he sighed. 'We'll learn to cope with that.'

His *trust* in her had been damaged. Not his love for her, or his need of her, only his trust. It wasn't much of a foundation for marriage. But what else did they have?

'I can't sleep with you, Raff,' she looked at him

unblinkingly. 'You see, although you doubt me when I say Court has only ever been a dear friend to me, I know the truth, and your lack of faith in *me* has badly shaken my trust in *you*!'

He gave an abrupt inclination of his head. 'I understand your reasons for choosing to keep your own room, but maybe in time even that physical closeness will come back again. For the moment, we're starting again from the beginning, like strangers.'

'I think our son or daughter might have something to say about that!'

Raff returned her teasing smile, the two of them sharing a brief moment of camaraderie. And as he smiled Bryna realised how strained he had looked until that moment, the leanness of his body and the lines about his eyes revealing that he was just as unhappy as she.

'Well, *almost* like strangers,' he mocked. 'Have I told you how much being pregnant suits you?' he added huskily.

They both knew he hadn't, that he had rarely spoken to her at all since her pregnancy began to show. Her blush of pleasure at the compliment added a glow to her cheeks, and a sparkle to her eyes.

She wasn't to know, as she smiled at him shyly, that Raff's trust in her would be tested sooner than she would have wished!

Their relationship didn't change overnight; there was still a strain between them that couldn't be banished no matter how much they talked and

laughed and spent time together. And they did a lot
of those things during the next few weeks, often
managing to lunch together as well as being
together in the evenings.

They were closer to being friends now than they
had ever been, having become lovers so quickly in
the first place that they hadn't really taken the time
to get to know each other as well as they probably
should have done. Now they had time to discover
the things they had in common, and surprisingly
enough they found that was quite a lot. Raff even
began to discuss his work with her, something she
had thought he would never do.

And yet that underlying strain persisted between
them.

It was physical rather than mental, Bryna either
withdrawing or trembling almost uncontrollably if
Raff should touch her, and she could feel his tension
if she should accidentally touch him in any way.

They wanted each other.

They had gone back to the beginning, started
again, had formed a sort of friendship, and now
they wanted each other so badly it was starting to
affect that very friendship they had striven for.

Bryna was more confused than ever; she had no
idea where it would all end.

But she was grateful that the two of them were at
least friends enough to be able to accept Kate's
invitation to dinner in the certainty that they
wouldn't cause any friction by their presence. The
young girl had given them a formal invitation to
what she called her belated moving-dinner-party,
and Raff had accepted just as formally.

'I just hope she's learnt to cook since the time she served up rice pudding and potatoes!' he said ruefully on the drive over to the flat. 'Together!'

Bryna laughed softly at the disgusting concoction. 'How old was she then?'

'Nine,' he grimaced. 'She was trying to act the "little mother" after Josey died, and Paul and I ate it because we didn't want to hurt her feelings.'

Bryna smiled. 'Well, I think she has more of an idea now; she was very helpful when we all cooked the Christmas dinner.'

'Let's hope so,' her father drawled. 'You look lovely tonight, Bryna.' He laced the fingers of her right hand with his.

So did he! He had always been handsome to her, but this last few weeks he had become even more so, so that she only had to look at him to feel her heart beat faster and her mouth go dry. And in an evening suit Raff could only be described as devastating! She knew she was suffering from frustration, that Raff could have been wearing patched denims and she would still have wanted him, but she couldn't help the way he made her feel breathless just to look at him.

And his compliment about her own appearance was very welcome. At nineteen weeks her pregnancy was almost halfway through, and her waistline had expanded to match that. None of her normal clothing fitted her any more, and although the maternity wardrobe Raff had insisted on buying her was very attractive she still didn't feel exactly glamorous in the flowing blue dress, and she needed Raff's compliment as a bolster to her flagging self-confidence about the way she looked to him and others.

Especially when she saw the dress Brenda was wearing! The tall redhead was very attractive, but even so the low-cut black dress seemed to be a little old for her eighteen years.

Kate gave her father and Bryna an apologetic grimace as she moved to pour them a drink. 'I only got it in for the occasion,' she hastened to explain at her father's raised brows.

'I hope so,' he murmured before turning to her flatmate. 'You're looking very sophisticated to-night, Brenda,' he told her smoothly.

Bryna watched ruefully as the young girl took the politeness as an invitation to flirt with him, knowing by the embarrassed flush to Kate's cheeks that she could cheerfully have strangled the other girl.

'I'll help you out in the kitchen,' Bryna offered gently, not at all perturbed about Brenda's obvious behaviour; the only thing she knew she could be sure of was that Raff wasn't interested in a college friend of his daughter!

'She's incredible!' muttered Kate as she banged about in the kitchen putting the finishing touches to the meal. 'I asked her to behave tonight, and she promised she would, and within a few seconds of Daddy's arrival she's throwing herself all over him!'

Bryna laughed softly at Kate's obvious disgust with her friend. 'I shouldn't worry about it, your father is only playing with her.'

'*We* all know that,' grumbled Kate, her pretty face flushed with anger. 'But Brenda doesn't know how to take no for an answer!'

Obviously the last weeks of sharing a flat with the other girl had opened Kate's eyes to Brenda's selfish nature. 'How's the flat-sharing going?' Bryna enquired casually.

'Oh, you know,' Kate turned away, shrugging. 'We get on okay together.'

Quite a turn-about from thinking Brenda was the most wonderful friend in the world, but Bryna wisely kept her thoughts to herself. She felt sure Kate felt badly enough about her father being proved right about the other girl without adding salt to the wound.

By the time they returned to the lounge Paul and his girl-friend, Lynn, had arrived with Kate's friend Roger and another young man known to them all as Flip, who appeared to be Brenda's date for the evening, although he certainly wasn't the same young man Bryna had seen emerge from Brenda's bedroom that day!

Bryna was sure Raff felt as out of place with these six youngsters as she was starting to!

The doorbell rang again shortly before eight, and Kate jumped up to answer it. 'Just so that you two wouldn't feel as if you'd been asked along to act as chaperons,' she told them teasingly before going to the door.

Bryna's sense of foreboding had warned her who the late arrival was even before Court came into the room at Kate's side. She looked pleadingly at Raff, knowing by the way he tensed that he was ready to demand that the other man leave—or he would.

Then he turned slightly and met her pleading

gaze, and some of the coldness left him as he followed her gaze to Kate's excited face. His daughter wanted both him and the other man here, and for either of them to leave would upset Kate. Raff relaxed slightly although his eyes remained dangerously narrowed.

'Look who's here!' Kate laughed her pleasure at this last arrival. 'Poor Uncle Court's date had a migraine and couldn't come,' she added sympathetically, her arm looped through his.

'And you couldn't come up with a replacement even though it was short notice?' mocked Raff, the hardness of his eyes telling of his intention to wound. 'You do disappoint me, Court,' he drawled.

Court met his gaze challengingly. 'I thought that with all the beautiful ladies here you gentlemen wouldn't mind sharing!'

Bryna winced at the barb. Court was angry at Raff's behaviour and he had a right to be, but the situation was rapidly spiralling out of control. Surprisingly it was Kate who smoothed the tense atmosphere.

'You can sit next to me, Uncle Court,' she told him lightly.

He gave her a wolfish grin. 'In that case you'd better stop calling me Uncle!'

Roger put his arm possessively about Kate's shoulders. 'She only said you could *sit* next to her,' he smiled.

Kate blushed at his obvious claim to her, glancing awkwardly at her father.

Bryna looked at Raff too, relieved to see that there was humour in his eyes now. Knowing how possessive *he* was of Kate she had feared his reaction to another man showing such proprietorial rights. But she should have known he didn't disapprove of the pleasant Roger Delaney. Tall and dark, with warm blue eyes, the younger man was studying to become a history teacher, and Raff obviously like him.

Bryna watched Raff now as he crossed the room to her side, stiffening a little as his arm curved possessively about her own waist to rest his hand against their child.

'You should have found a replacement, Court,' he drawled. 'None of us is willing to share.' He looked at the other man challengingly.

'Flip doesn't mind.' Brenda gave Court a glowing smile as she pressed against him.

Flip didn't have to mind, it soon became obvious. He was a quiet young man, obviously dazzled by the vivacity of his date, and it soon became apparent to all but him that Brenda had only invited him so that *she* wouldn't be the one without a partner for the evening. Now that Court had arrived alone she more or less ignored poor Flip, monopolising a bemused Court during the meal.

Bryna did her best to include Flip in the conversation, feeling the need to keep talking herself when, for the most part, Raff remained broodingly silent.

She knew he was angry about Court's presence here, but that for Kate's sake he was making an effort not to actually say anything in case he forgot this was supposed to be a happy occasion and insulted Court as he obviously longed to do. She

only hoped that he didn't think she had known of
Court's presence here tonight, because she hadn't;
she would never have willingly placed herself in this
tension-filled situation. The doctor was pleased
with her pregnancy so far, although her blood-
pressure's habit of fluctuating up and down did
cause him some concern. And she was sure tonight
couldn't be doing much to ease that situation!

The pity of it was that she and Raff had come so
far from the first cold weeks of their marriage.
There was true friendship between them now, a
sharing, something they had never had before. She
didn't want to lose all that now just because they
had been forced to endure an evening of Court's
company.

'I'm sorry.'

She looked at Court questioningly as he joined
her on the sofa during the brief time Raff left her to
get her a glass of orange juice, looking around
quickly to see if Raff were watching them now. Her
panicked gazed clashed with his unreadable one as
he stood across the room, and hers softened
pleadingly.

Court sighed. 'I should never have come here
tonight.' He was shaking his head as Bryna turned
back to him. 'I wasn't going to because I knew you
and Raff would be here too, but Kate was so
insistent.'

Bryna gave him a sympathetic smile, knowing
that if any damage were to be done to her new-
found relationship with Raff it would already have
happened; and she couldn't do a thing about it.
'How have you been?'

'Fine,' Court nodded. 'And you are obviously blooming.'

'Yes,' she gave a self-conscious laugh.

He looked at her searchingly. 'How are you really, Bryna?' he asked quietly. 'I've been worried about you since that day in the restaurant, but you didn't call me again . . .!' He shrugged.

'There was no need,' she dismissed the apprehension she had known that night as she waited for Raff, still believing he would never have physically harmed her.

'So you and Raff are okay now?' Court probed.

She gave a rueful shrug. 'About as okay as we'll ever be, I think,' she nodded.

He looked at her searchingly. 'And are you happy?'

Yes, she was happy. Not in an ecstatic way, but the new understanding she and Raff had come to in recent weeks had filled her with an inner tranquillity, an acceptance that he was giving her as much of himself as he was able, even if it wasn't the love she still craved from him.

She looked across the room at him anxiously now as she realised how long it was taking him to come back with her drink; he was deep in conversation with Roger Delaney, seemingly unaware of the two of them seated together on the sofa. And yet despite that Bryna knew he was very much aware of them.

'Yes,' she assured Court unhesitatingly.

'Hm. In that case, are you going to mind if I talk about Raff's suspicions concerning the two of us?' Court looked worried.

Some of the warmth left her eyes, but she shook

her head. 'If you have anything new to tell me I'd be glad to hear it.'

Court frowned. 'Well, the idea came to me when I saw him with Raff in the restaurant that day. I did notice him a couple of times while we were out together, and a few digs from him would——'

'From who?' she demanded impatiently.

'Raff's assistant. What's his name—?—Hillier,' he remembered. 'A couple of times when we were out together I noticed him at the same restaurant. I thought it was a coincidence, but you did say Raff had accused us of being *seen* together, and I suppose Hillier could have been the one spying on us.'

'Why on earth would he do that?' Bryna asked disbelievingly.

'I don't know,' Court shook his head. 'But he's the only one I can think of who actually saw us together.'

Stuart Hillier? She had never liked the man, but even so . . . !

Unless Raff had asked the other man to follow her? He had had her followed once, so why not then? He had denied having her followed then, of course, but surely it was too much of a coincidence to be one.

'You think he told Raff about us?' she said weakly, knowing by the compassion in Court's eyes that he had also guessed what she couldn't put into words, that Raff had *asked* his assitant to spy on them!

'Don't you?' he said gently.

'Yes.' She turned away, blinking back the tears, the trust and genuine liking she and Raff had built up in recent weeks crumbling as she knew it had been built on a lie. God, she felt ill when she thought now of the times she had ached to ask Raff to make their marriage a real one!

'I'm sorry, Bryna,' Court clasped her hand in his, 'I just thought it was something you should know.'

She was glad she did; she had wanted Raff so badly on the drive over here that she had been going to make the first move towards a normal marriage when they got home. Oh, what a fool she had been these last few weeks! Raff didn't want a friendship with her, he had just taken the doctor's advice that a 'happy and contented mother made for an uncomplicated pregnancy' so seriously he had been willing to forget their differences until at least her pregnancy was over. And then what? Would they go back to the coldness, the indifference?

'Here you are, Bryna.' Raff appeared back at her side with her drink after deliberately leaving her alone with Court, she felt sure; he had been testing her. 'Darling, you're very pale,' he added frowningly.

Darling. And the concern. *All false!* 'I think I'd like to go home now, if you don't mind,' she said bluntly.

He looked at the other man with narrowed eyes. 'Of course,' he agreed automatically. 'I'll tell Kate we're leaving.'

'I may be wrong, Bryna,' Court encouraged once they were alone. 'As you said, why would Hillier want to do something like that?'

They both knew why, because Raff had *asked* him to!

Bryna didn't remember saying her goodbyes and thanks to Kate, but she supposed she must have done, as she received no strange looks at their departure.

The easy camaraderie that had existed between herself and Raff on the drive over to Kate's flat was noticeably lacking on the journey back to their home; Bryna was lost in a sea of misery, and Raff's thoughts were grim, if his expression was anything to go by.

'Kate does seem to have more idea of what to serve at a dinner party now.' Raff's abrupt comment suddenly broke the silence.

The avocado with prawns, followed by chicken in white wine sauce, and then a delicious array of sweets, had been very enjoyable. 'It was very nice,' Bryna replied curtly.

'What did you think of Roger Delaney?'

'He seems very nice,' she shrugged.

'Yes,' he acknowledged tersely.

Bryna waited tensely for the question concerning her conversation with Court.

But it never came, Raff once again lapsing into silence.

Bryna went straight up the stairs to her room as soon as they got home, leaving Raff to lock up. She sensed his searching gaze on her as she walked up the stairs, her back ramrod-straight as she refused to turn around and meet that puzzled gaze.

She wasn't in the least surprised at his entrance to her bedroom minutes later after the briefest of knocks; she had probably been expecting it as she sat in her bedroom chair, still wearing her coat.

'Let me help you.' Raff stood her up to remove the coat and unzip her dress, turning her back to face him to slide the dress down her body. Bryna offered him no resistance, and he looked at her searchingly as he removed her silky underwear. 'What did Court say to upset you?' he finally rasped the question she had been waiting for.

She stood naked before him, and it didn't seem to matter, that intense awareness of him that had been with her in recent weeks had completely gone in the face of his deceit. 'Nothing,' she claimed flatly.

Raff's mouth tightened. 'He must have said something, you were all right until he spoke to you!'

'Was I?' she said dully.

'Yes, damn it!' He clasped her upper arms. 'Bryna, look at me!'

She raised lids that suddenly seemed too heavy. He looked the same as he always did, arrogantly handsome, totally in command. And for the first time since she had met him he left her cold.

'Bryna!' his voice deepened in desperation as he seemed to look into her eyes and see the complete vacuum of her emotions. 'I want you, Bryna,' he shook her slightly. 'I want you!'

'I'm not stopping you taking me,' she told him uninterestedly.

'God!' he groaned, his frown pained. 'Bryna?' He shook her again, giving a low groan as he bent his head to claim her lips as if by compulsion.

Emotionally he hadn't been able to reach her, but as the kiss went on and on, and his hands roamed almost desperately over the nakedness of her body, she felt her defences begin to crack, to crumble, and finally to be completely forgotten.

She was disgusted with her weakness even as she gloried in his lovemaking. It had been so long since she had known the ecstasy of his touch, and her body cried out for the fulfilment it knew only this man could give her.

She thought she would collapse completely as she felt his hand against the swelling of her body that was their child, feeling the baby stir in answer to its father's touch. The baby knew, as she did, that they were possessions of this man, to do with as he would. And if he chose to make love to her she couldn't stop him; she knew that she wanted him too.

His body was hard and yet warmly inviting as he moved above her as they lay on the bed, his clothes long ago thrown to the floor, and Bryna groaned her pleasure as they became one, arching her hips to meet his, needing to drive the demons of doubt from her mind even as she needed Raff's fierce thrusts inside her.

The weeks without each other took their toll on their control, and their pleasure was over almost before it had begun, although it was more intense than anything Bryna had ever known before. She revelled in Raff's release as he trembled above and within her.

Finally he found the strength to lie beside her, ever careful of their child. 'Now tell me what Court said to upset you,' he prompted huskily.

She had known, despite their lovemaking, that the question had only been postponed, not forgotten, and now that some measure of sanity had been returned to her she looked at him steadily. 'Was Stuart Hillier the one who told you I had been meeting Court?'

Raff frowned. 'What difference does it make who told me?'

'It matters to me,' she bit out. 'Was it him?' She sat up.

'I——'

'Oh, my God!' Dizziness swept over her as she looked at the bed between them, a dark red staining the cream sheet. 'I'm bleeding, Raff,' she looked at him with panicked eyes. 'I'm losing our baby!'

CHAPTER NINE

'THE doctor says about a week's rest here,' Raff told her grimly. 'And then you can probably come home. Also to rest,' he added determinedly.

Bryna voiced no complaint as she lay in the hospital bed. She knew she would stay here for the whole of the next twenty-one weeks as long as it meant her baby could be born healthy and safe at the end of it.

Raff had lost no time when he saw the truth of her distressed cry, dressing hurriedly before wrapping her in a blanket to carry her down to the car and drive her to the hospital.

They had been here almost two hours now, while the doctors stopped the flow of blood and established whether or not she had gone into premature labour. She hadn't, and the bleeding had also stopped, for now.

Raff had been beside her the whole time, and if the emergency staff at this prestigious hospital had found anything strange about his carrying his naked, obviously pregnant, wife in to them they hadn't shown it, but had worked quietly and calmly to make sure that she didn't lose her child.

And all the time that they had Bryna had known that before she made her horrific discovery she had seen the truth in Raff's eyes; Stuart Hillier *had* been the one to tell him she was meeting Court behind his back.

'I'm sorry.'

She looked up at Raff in surprise, startled by the anguish in his voice. He looked pained, under severe strain; the last few hours had taken their toll on him too. 'It's over now,' she dismissed distantly.

'God, I hope so!' He clasped her hand in his, looking strangely unreal dressed as he was in the evening clothes he had grabbed up off the floor to pull on before bringing her here. 'I should never have made love to you.'

For different reasons Bryna agreed with him. Making love with him had shown her that no matter how much he hurt her she loved him too much to ever say no to him. She had never believed herself to have masochistic tendencies, but surely loving Raff in the mindless way that she did had to be that!

'It wasn't that—the doctor said so.' She blushed as she recalled the embarrassingly intimate questions the young doctor had asked her; it seemed that when you had a baby privacy became a thing of the past! 'It's my blood-pressure,' she reminded Raff.

Raff shook his head. 'It was seeing Court again that did it——'

'It was knowing you would take the lies of a man you barely know over the truth of your wife!' she cut in on his angry tirade with one of her own, her eyes deeply purple.

Raff's jaw clenched. 'I don't think we should argue about this now——'

'I don't think we should argue about it all,' she bit

out caustically. 'You've already made your decision about who's telling the truth, and I know you're wrong. Stalemate. Now I believe the doctor said I should rest . . .' she added pointedly.

Raff's cheeks became flushed at her dismissal. 'If only you would let me explain——'

'I don't have to do anything but rest now, remember?' She looked at him coldly.

He sighed his defeat. 'Bryna, I—I care for you. If anything had happened to you——'

'You mean the baby,' she corrected harshly. 'But don't worry, Raff, I probably want this baby more than you do.' Because it was probably the only child she would ever have. Conceiving had been difficult enough, but now that she was pregnant her body still seemed to be rebelling.

His eyes darkened. 'I doubt if that's possible,' his voice was husky. 'Get some sleep now.' He bent to kiss her brow, drawing back quickly as she flinched. 'I want the baby to be all right,' he rasped. 'But God, how I wish you'd never become pregnant!'

Bryna's chin went back defensively. 'Believe me, if I'd thought there'd been a possibility that I *could* conceive I wouldn't have chosen you as the father!' As soon as she had made the heated statement she regretted it, sure that Raff would twist her words in some way so that he could think even more badly of her. She had never meant to tell him that she had believed herself barren, but her temper had got the better of her.

Raff became suddenly still. 'What do you mean?'

'It doesn't matter——'

'*What do you mean!*'

She swallowed hard, meeting his gaze unflinchingly. 'I had an operation in my teens that made the doctors tell my parents at the time that I would never have a child,' she dismissed carelessly. 'I didn't use any form of birth control during our affair, Raff, because I didn't think I could become pregnant!'

He drew back to drop down into the chair drawn up beside her bed. 'I thought perhaps you didn't like children, that like actually living together, they were too much of a commitment. I never guessed . . .' He looked at her sharply. 'And instead it was Court who was sterile.'

'Yes, what a pair we would have made,' she acknowledged bitterly.

'Is that why——?'

'What?' she probed warily as he broke off abruptly, his jaw tight, his mouth thinned. 'Why what, Raff?' she pressured.

He drew in a ragged breath. 'Why you chose me that day and not Court.'

She could feel herself pale. 'I didn't choose you, *you* chose me,' she choked out hardly. 'And I was hardly likely to have asked Court if he was capable of fathering a child before deciding whether or not to go out with him, just *in case* the doctors were wrong after all and I could conceive!'

'No, of course not,' Raff accepted self-disgustedly. 'I don't know what's the matter with me. I——'

'I do,' she scorned. 'You're determined to think the worst of me, to believe I had some ulterior motive for going out with you at all, for marrying

you. Well, maybe this will help,' she snapped. 'I
never *would* have married you if I hadn't been
frightened you would take my baby from me!' She
was breathing hard in her agitation, glaring up at
him.

A nerve pulsed in his cheek. 'I——'

'I'm sorry, Mr Gallagher,' a pretty nurse murmured smoothly as she entered the private room.
'But Mrs Gallagher should be resting now. You too,'
she encouraged gently. 'It's two o'clock in the
morning! And from my experience, fathers-to-be
need as much rest as the mother!' She frowned
when her teasing didn't even arouse a rueful smile.
'The danger is over now, Mr and Mrs Gallagher,'
she comforted softly.

The danger was over, but so was her marriage;
Bryna knew now it should never have begun, that
instead of taking what she had believed was the
only way, she should have fought Raff in court. She
wanted to tell him so now, but as the nurse
continued to hover pointedly in her room she knew
it would have to wait until another time, when they
were alone.

But they never were alone. She didn't think it was
through Raff's design, but each time he visited her
he had either Kate or Paul with him, the two of
them very concerned about her and the welfare of
their brother or sister. The scare had succeeded in
bringing them closer to their sibling, at least.

She had plenty of other visitors too. Her worried
parents came down from Scotland, several of the
models and friends she worked with popped in for a
few minutes, Gilly, and once Court arrived just

before the regular visiting time, obviously so that he should avoid running into Raff.

'For you, because they remind me of your eyes.' He put a posy of violets on the bed.

Bryna stroked the delicate petals, blinking up at him tearfully. 'Thank you.'

'Hey, I came here to cheer you up, not make you cry!' He pulled up a chair and sat down, grinning amiably. 'What's the food like?'

'The food?' she laughed. She couldn't help it!

'I've always been told it's one of the first questions you should ask a person in hospital,' Court explained. 'I've heard that the food is atrocious in these places. I could have something exotic sent in——'

'The food is fine,' chuckled Bryna. 'How did you know where I was?' she asked curiously.

'Kate,' he supplied ruefully. 'She told me about the scare you all had. How are you feeling now?'

There had been no more bleeding, her blood-pressure had steadied, and the doctor seemed very pleased with her. 'I was a little scared when it happened,' she admitted 'But everything seems fine now.'

He suddenly looked older, his expression strained. 'I couldn't bear it if anything I'd said or done had caused you to lose the baby.'

'You haven't, and I didn't,' she reassured him, knowing exactly why he would be so upset if he should be the cause of harm coming to her child. Poor Court! 'Court, when—when the baby is born I would like you to be its godfather.'

His brows rose. 'And what would Raff have to say about that?'

'Nothing,' her mouth firmed, 'because it will be none of his business.'

His brows rose at the vehemence in her voice. 'You've left him?' he sounded puzzled.

'I—— Not yet,' she moistened dry lips. 'I haven't had the opportunity to tell him yet, but I—I will. And I want you to be the baby's godfather.'

Court looked at her searchingly, his eyes dark with pain. 'He told you, didn't he,' he said flatly.

She had blundered and hurt him, and that was something she had never meant to do. 'Court——'

'It's all right.' He stood up, his face strangely expressionless now. 'Knowing what Raff believes about us, and the existence of your pregnancy, I can imagine under what circumstances he told you.' He drew a ragged breath. 'I have to go now——'

'Oh, Court, no!' she pleaded with him, reaching out to him imploringly. 'I'm so sorry. The last thing I wanted to do was hurt you——'

'You haven't,' he told her abruptly. 'I came to terms with my sterility years ago,' he added bitterly.

'Most women would be happy to adopt a baby just to have you as their husband——'

'Most women!' he scorned. 'I think you're overestimating the majority of your sex, Bryna.'

She swallowed hard. 'And so you've decided not to marry at all,' she guessed, having made much the same decision herself once she accepted how her own infertility made her feel.

'I didn't make the decision,' Court rasped. 'It was made for me.'

'But, Court, there are lots of women nowadays who don't even want children——'

'Selfish, egotistical women who don't want to ruin their figure or their careers,' he cut in disgustedly. 'I don't want a wife like that.'

She shook her head. 'They aren't all like that, some of them——'

'Am I interrupting anything?' Alyson stood hesitantly in the doorway, her eyes lighting up with pleasure as she looked at the man she had found so fascinating at Bryna's wedding, glowingly beautiful as she came into the room, her black-haired, green-eyed beauty making her very photogenic. 'You didn't call me after the wedding,' she flirted with Court.

Some of the tension left his body as he smiled ruefully at Bryna before grinning wickedly at Alyson. 'Tonight?'

'Lovely,' Alyson gave him an enticing smile.

He nodded, his expression sobering as he turned to Bryna. 'Take care of yourself and the baby.'

'You aren't leaving?' she realised in dismay; they still had so much to say to each other.

His mouth twisted derisively. 'I think I'd better go before Raff gets here.'

'Oh, but——'

'Goodbye, Bryna.' He bent to kiss her cheek. 'Be happy.'

It sounded like a final parting! 'Court, you——'

He turned briefly at the door. 'I really do have to go,' he told her gruffly. 'Don't worry about me, Bryna,' he drawled as she still looked upset. 'I get by.' He looked pointedly at Alyson before leaving.

Bryna sat back wearily. The last thing she had wanted to do was hurt Court. Between the two of them she and Raff had hurt Court very much.

'*Did* I interrupt something?' Alyson looked concerned as she sat next to the bed, placing the magazines she had brought with her on the bedside table.

Bryna shook off her mood of despondency with an effort, smiling at her friend. 'No, of course not,' she dismissed lightly.

'Only Court seemed a little upset,' Alyson still frowned. 'Not at all like the charming rake I was so attracted to at your wedding.'

Bryna gave a disbelieving laugh. 'You think he's a rake, but you still asked him to call you!'

'Of course,' her friend grimaced. 'He'll be a welcome relief after that self-opinionated creep I *did* get a call from,' she grimaced.

She and Alyson had begun their modelling careers together eight years ago, and unluckily for Alyson, there seemed to have been a lot of 'creeps' during that time.

Bryna shook her head. 'You always did choose the wrong men.'

'You could have warned me,' Alyson complained. 'Then I wouldn't have had to endure that disaster of a date with him.'

'How could I have prevented that?' mocked Bryna.

'Well, I know he only works for your husband, but you must have realised by now what a creep he is!' Alyson said with feeling.

Bryna had stiffened just at the mention of Raff,

but as Alyson's words became clear she felt herself pale. 'Stuart Hillier called you?' she gasped.

'Yes.' Alyson wrinkled her lovely nose tellingly.

He wouldn't, Raff *wouldn't* . . .! 'He didn't give any indication at the wedding that he was attracted to you.' Bryna said dully.

'That's what I thought,' her friend grimaced. 'His call came completely out of the blue. In fact, I had trouble placing him at first. Then I realised he was the one who was attracted to you——'

'Oh, I don't think so,' Bryna protested instantly.

'Well, he certainly couldn't take his eyes off you.' Alyson shrugged. 'But after all, it was me he called. And he's quite attractive . . . If only he weren't such a bore.' She wrinkled her nose again.

'He talked about himself a lot?' prompted Bryna, not wanting to hear how Stuart Hillier had watched her constantly at the wedding.

'He talked about *Raff* a lot,' Alyson grimaced. 'I find your husband as attractive as the rest of the female population,' she sighed. 'But he *is* your husband, and while I'm on a date with another man I'd prefer to talk about something a little more—personal.'

Bryna wasn't sure if she was breathing any more. 'And me, did Stuart talk about me too?'

Her friend frowned. 'A couple of times,' she replied thoughtfully. 'Nothing detrimental,' she hastened to add. 'I wouldn't have allowed that. He mainly asked questions I thought he had no right to. I told him to ask Raff if he was that interested in you, and that seemed to shut him up!'

Because he didn't need to ask Raff anything

when he was the one that had prompted Stuart to ask Alyson the questions in the first place!

Raff had gone too far this time. Challenging her with his nonsensical accusations was one thing, alienating his best friend was another thing he was going to have to live with, but persuading her friends to talk about her was something else entirely.

It couldn't go on.

She forced herself to give Alyson a bright smile. 'Believe me, Court is much nicer than Stuart Hillier.'

Alyson gave a smile of anticipation. 'I certainly hope so!'

The two of them were still chatting together when Raff arrived a few minutes later. And for once he was alone. Bryna didn't try to stop Alyson leaving when she excused herself a few minutes later, although she did thank her for the magazines and for finding the time to come and see her, knowing how busy her friend was running the agency in her absence.

Raff placed the books and box of chocolates he had brought next to the magazines. 'It was nice of her to come,' he said lightly.

Bryna looked at him coldly. He was thinner, his cheeks hollow, his eyes lacking their usual brightness; she only wished it were his guilty conscience making him look that way. But she knew it wasn't. Raff didn't have a conscience to feel guilty with.

'Yes,' she bit out.

'Kate and Paul will be along later; they went to buy you a present.' He stood awkwardly beside the bed, making no effort to sit down as her other visitors had done.

'There's really no need for them to buy me something every time they come to see me,' she shook her head.

'This one is a welcome home present.' Raff's eyes blazed his satisfaction. 'I've just seen the doctor, he said you can come home tomorrow!'

She knew all about her proposed discharge from the hospital; she had discussed it with the doctor herself when he had visited her this morning. 'Yes,' she confirmed unenthusiastically.

Raff frowned at her tone. 'You don't sound very pleased about it.'

'Being discharged means that the danger to the baby is over, and I'm very pleased about that,' she insisted evenly.

'Then what's wrong?' He looked at her searchingly.

Bryna drew in a deep breath, knowing this wasn't going to be pleasant, but determined to go through with it. 'I'm not coming home,' she told him flatly.

Raff looked taken aback. 'But the doctor said that you're well enough to leave, that there's been no more bleeding, that——'

'I know exactly what the doctor said,' she cut in firmly. 'When I said I wasn't coming home, I meant to *your* home.' She met his gaze challengingly as his head went back in protest.

'It's *our* home, damn you,' he finally bit out gratingly. 'And where else would you go?'

She shrugged. 'Back to Scotland, to my parents——'

'You aren't well enough to travel,' he rasped.

She knew that, but she had hoped Raff wouldn't. She should have known better! But she hadn't really had time to think all her plans through yet. All she did know was that she had to get away from Raff.

'Then perhaps my mother could continue to stay on here and we could get a flat——'

'You know your father is having difficulty coping at home without your mother, that it's a busy time of year for them,' Raff dismissed. 'Besides, you don't have a flat any more.'

Her cheeks flushed in her agitation. 'I could rent one——'

'You aren't strong enough to shop for furnishings,' he bit out grimly.

'Then I'll rent a furnished one,' she told him desperately. 'But I am not living with you!' she glared at him, breathing hard.

'Calm down,' he instructed authoritatively. 'Do you want your blood-pressure to shoot up again?'

'No,' she conceded tightly. 'But our marriage is over, Raff. I want nothing more to do with you.'

A nerve pulsed in his jaw, fury glittering in his eyes. 'Do you have to move out for that?' he demanded finally.

Puzzlement darkened her eyes as she looked at him questioningly.

He gave an impatient shrug. 'We managed to live together all right the last time we ignored each other's existence!'

Bryna shook her head. 'I'm not sure I'll be able to do that this time,' she snapped.

'Why not?' he rasped.

'Because I don't trust you,' she scorned.

Raff's mouth tightened. 'I'm hardly likely to risk the life of my child by upsetting you again!'

'We married because of the baby, we agreed that would be all it was, but you broke your promise almost as soon as we were married,' she reminded him tautly. 'I can't trust you,' she repeated flatly.

'You can!' he grated. 'I give you my word I won't come near you or try to touch you again. I just want to take care of you. Let me take care of you,' his voice gentled.

She didn't want to do it, she wanted to get as far away from him and his continuous spying on her, but she knew she never would. 'You said you would stay away from me!' She looked at him with narrowed eyes.

'I will,' he agreed heavily. 'But I have staff at the house who can look after you, make sure that you don't overdo things. And you know it would only worry your parents if you asked your mother to stay on any longer than she already has.'

Her parents had both come down as soon as they knew she had been admitted to hospital, but her father had had to return to Scotland after a couple of days. Having convinced both her parents that both she and the baby were fine now, she knew it would only upset them if she left Raff now.

'I don't even want to see you, Raff,' she told him coldly. 'And once the baby is born I'm finding a place of my own.'

His mouth tightened over the last, but he said nothing, nodding acceptance of her conditions.

CHAPTER TEN

SHE had only been back in the house a few days
when Kate arrived with her suitcase in her hand.

Bryna put down the book she was reading to look
anxiously at her stepdaughter as she dropped the
suitcase down on the floor to run sobbing across the
lounge. Bryna opened her arms to the girl,
murmuring words of soothing comfort as she
stroked the glossy black curls while waiting for the
tears to stop.

Kate finally gave a last shuddering sob and
moved back out of Bryna's arms. She looked so
young and vulnerable that Bryna's heart went out to
her.

'What happened?' she prompted gently.

Kate shook her head, wiping away the tears with
her fingertips. 'I shouldn't be worrying you in your
condition——'

'My "condition" at the moment is that of being
your stand-in mother,' chided Bryna. 'I care about
you, Kate.'

'I care about you, too,' the girl gave a watery
smile. 'And I do think of you as my mother, but Paul
and I decided you're too young to have us call you
Mum. We thought you could be our big sister
instead.'

Bryna wasn't upset that Kate and Paul had
decided on the latter; the fact that her stepchildren

had discussed the possibility of calling her 'Mum' and only vetoed it because of her age filled her with a warm glow. 'Big sisters are for confiding in,' she encouraged softly.

Kate grimaced. 'It's Brenda!' she said with feeling.

Bryna had an idea that it might be, in fact she was surprised Kate had lasted the two months that she had with the other girl. 'Do you want to tell me about it?' she prompted lightly.

Kate stood up restlessly. 'Why not?' she said disgustedly. 'I thought she was my friend,' her eyes blazed darkly grey. 'But she isn't,' she scorned. 'She doesn't know the meaning of the word friendship!'

The presence of the suitcase, and Kate's obvious anger, implied that the disagreement between the two girls was serious. 'Did Brenda do something you disapprove of?' Bryna probed.

'Oh, I could accept her untidiness, her selfishness, even the men she occasionally had staying overnight with her.' Kate blushed as she revealed the latter. 'But I can't, and I *won't*, accept her trying to seduce Roger!'

It was worse than Bryna had expected, knowing how much Kate liked Roger; her affection for him had been obvious on the occasions he had accompanied Kate to see her over the last ten days.

'Did she succeed?' Bryna asked reluctantly.

'Of course not!' Kate defended indignantly. 'Roger isn't interested in her, he lo— well, it's me he likes,' she amended blushingly. 'He's as disgusted by her behaviour as I am.'

Bryna could imagine that he was, but she had felt

the question had to be asked. She was glad, for Kate's sake, that Roger's affection was as deep as her own for him. 'What exactly happened?' she frowned.

'I was late getting out of my class this evening, and Roger thought I must have already left, and went straight to the flat. I walked in just as Brenda was trying to kiss him while he tried to fight her off!' Her eyes glittered angrily with remembered outrage. 'I watched them as he succeeded, wiping the touch of her lips from his mouth with the back of his hand while he told her to stay away from him, that he wasn't interested. Of course, as soon as Brenda saw me she claimed that Roger had attacked her, but I'd *seen* them! I packed my case and left. I'll get the rest of my things later. I just had to get away from there.' She shuddered.

'And where is Roger now?'

Kate looked uncomfortable. 'He wanted to come home with me, but I—I told him I'd see him later. I think I should face Daddy alone,' she added with obvious reluctance for the idea.

Bryna's mouth firmed as she guessed the reason for Kate's reluctance was that she dreaded the idea of her father saying 'I told you so'.

Raff had kept completely to his word this time, spending his evenings in his study, not even bothering to say hello to her when he arrived home at night. And she liked it that way; she couldn't have even borne a distant politeness from him, feeling about him as she did now. But she was as unsure as Kate about the way he would react to

Kate's news, and she didn't think the girl should face him alone!

They both gave a startled jolt as the front door was slammed closed, Kate turning pleadingly to Bryna. 'That will be him now,' she grimaced. 'I think I've changed my mind about seeing him alone!'

Bryna gave a rueful smile. 'Don't worry, I'm not going anywhere.'

They were sitting together on the sofa as Raff strode past the lounge door on the way to his study as he usually did. The same pattern had been followed on the last three evenings, and Bryna had known that he wouldn't vary his routine. Usually he didn't even glance into the room he knew she occupied, but tonight he frowned and then stopped, turning slowly, his eyes widening as he saw Kate sitting with Bryna, Kate's suitcase standing between them and him.

Bryna looked from father to daughter, Raff's expression questioning, Kate looking as if she might begin to cry again. 'Kate has decided to come back home for a while,' she informed Raff lightly.

His eyes narrowed, and then he relaxed slightly, strolling into the room, dropping his briefcase down into a chair. 'That will be nice,' he murmured. 'How long can you stay, darling?' He poured himself a drink as the two women shook their heads at his offer.

'I—er—I——' Kate looked helplessly at Bryna.

She gave the girl a reassuring smile. 'The truth is, Raff, Kate has decided she'd like to move back with us and help keep me company until the baby is born. Isn't that nice of her?'

'Very,' he drawled. 'I'm sure Bryna appreciates your kindness, Kate,' he told his daughter warmly.

Kate blushed at the unmerited praise. 'I—I think I'll take my things upstairs and change for dinner.' She gave Bryna a grateful hug before hurrying from the room.

Raff sighed as the door closed behind her, suddenly looking weary. 'What really happened?'

Bryna sat tensely on the edge of the sofa now that the two of them were alone. This was the first time thay had spoken together since the morning Raff had driven her home from the hospital, the first time she had really looked at him in that time too. If he had looked ill three days ago he looked ten time worse now, his face gaunt, his eyes bruised and sunken, the looseness of his suit telling of his loss of weight.

'Bryna?' he frowned as he received no answer.

She drew in a ragged breath, dismissing any feelings of compassion for him that might have reared their silly head. This man was invincible, he needed no one's pity, least of all hers. 'Brenda flirted with one man too many,' she drawled. 'Roger,' she explained at his puzzled look.

'Oh,' he rasped.

'I'm sure Kate intends telling you about it, as soon as she calms down a little,' she said distantly. 'At the moment she's just very disillusioned.'

'About Roger?'

'About Brenda,' she corrected drily. 'Roger very firmly repulsed the over-confident Miss Sanders.'

'Thank God for that,' grimaced Raff, standing

close to the fireplace, the warmth the fire emitted
not seeming to bother him. 'I get the feeling Kate is
in love with him.'

Bryna didn't miss the half-question in his tone. 'I
think you would have to ask Kate about that,' she
evaded.

He nodded abruptly. 'Thank you for—well, for
being here when she needed someone to talk to.'

She looked at him searchingly. 'Why shouldn't I
be?' she finally answered him. 'I like both your
children, I always have.'

'It's just their father you can't stand to have near
you!' Raff swallowed some of the whisky in his
glass. 'You do realise that Kate's being here will
have to change all that?'

'What do you mean?' she asked warily, her hands
clenched.

He shrugged. 'We can hardly continue to act as
strangers with Kate back in the house.'

The last three days of peace and sanity faded as
she saw the truth of his words. The last thing she
wanted to do was upset Kate any further, by letting
her see the deterioration of her father's marriage to
Bryna, when she had already suffered such a blow
to her trust in people being what they seemed to be.
But neither could she pretend this was a happy
marriage.

'I'm willing to start taking my meals with you
again if it will help,' she accepted stiffly.

His mouth tightened. 'You would do that for
Kate but not for me?'

'You aren't vulnerable the way she is,' Bryna
snapped.

'I'm not?' he rasped self-derisively. 'Then why am I clinging on to a wife who's just waiting for the time she can leave me to be with the man she really loves?' His eyes were narrowed.

Bryna gasped. 'Not Court again!' she sighed her angry impatience. 'I haven't seen him since——' she broke off as she realised how recently she *had* seen him, a visit Raff knew nothing about.

'Four days ago,' Raff put in, softly contradicting that belief. 'I saw him come into your room that night,' he explained at her startled look. 'That was why I came in late,' he added grimly.

'You told me you'd been to see the doctor——'

'I'd seen him earlier,' he bit out.

'If you knew Court was in my room with me why didn't you——?'

'Walk in on the pair of you?' he finished bitterly. 'I had no wish to see the two of you together. It was enough that you told me you were leaving me when I did get in to see you!'

'But that had nothing to do with my having seen Court, that was because——'

'Aren't you going to change, Daddy?' Kate bounced back into the room, her usual exuberance almost restored. 'I called Roger from upstairs and invited him over for dinner; he'll be here in a few minutes.'

Raff gave one last regretful glance at Bryna before smiling at his daughter. 'And when can I expect him to ask for my daughter's hand in marriage?' he teased her.

Kate blushed. 'We've already decided that we

aren't going to get married for a couple of years,' she told him awkwardly.

'I suppose I should be grateful you bothered to tell me even that,' her father said drily.

She grinned. 'I'm determined to wait until the baby is old enough to be either pageboy or bridesmaid!'

The laughter left Raff's eyes, although the smile remained on his lips. 'That may not be for some time,' he said drily.

Bryna knew from his expression that he doubted she or the baby would still be here then. But although she might have accepted banishment from his children's lives as well as his when their affair ended she had no intention of doing that now that she had been his wife and was having Kate's and Paul's brother or sister.

Kate shrugged, unaware of the tension of the adults. 'We have time. Do hurry up, Daddy,' she encouraged impatiently. 'I'm hungry!'

'You always were,' he shook his head ruefully. 'Maybe if I tell Roger how much you're going to cost to keep in food he'll change his mind about marrying you!' he teased before going upstairs.

Kate moved to hug Bryna a second time. 'Thank you so much for coming to my rescue like that earlier.'

'Your father guessed I wasn't telling the truth,' she grimaced.

'I knew he would,' Kate nodded. 'I'll talk to him about it later.'

For all that Bryna and Raff didn't exchange more than a couple of words it was a pleasantly lighthearted meal, Roger and Raff getting on just as well as they had in the past; Bryna was sure that when the time did come that Kate would have no difficulty at all in convincing her father of Roger's worth.

They returned to the lounge for coffee, Bryna pouring, glad to have something to do with her hands; the meal was a strain for her even if it had passed without incident.

'I'm so glad you and Uncle Court have resolved your differences,' Kate told her father happily. 'Whatever they were,' she added. 'You needn't look so surprised, Daddy, I'm well aware of the fact that the two of you haven't been the best of friends lately.'

That had to be an understatement, and Bryna looked questioningly at Raff; he hadn't given the impression earlier that he and Court were friends again.

He frowned at Kate. 'I didn't doubt your astuteness, I merely wondered what had given you the impression our "differences had been resolved",' he grated.

Kate's pleasure wavered a little. 'You mean they haven't?'

'No. Look, Kate,' he continued soothingly as her expression revealed her dismay. 'Arguments happen occasionally. We can't live happily-ever-after all the time——'

'I know that,' she dismissed scornfully. 'I just thought—hoped——'

'I don't know why you thought that,' he frowned. 'I haven't seen Court for a couple of weeks——'

'No, but Stuart has,' Kate cut in. 'And the only reason I could think of for him being with Uncle Court was if the two of you were setting up a business deal.'

Raff's eyes were narrowed. 'When did Stuart see Court?' he enquired quietly.

Kate shrugged. 'I saw them together a couple of weeks ago.'

Bryna had become very still. Court and Stuart Hillier? What possible reason could the two men have to meet if not on Raff's behalf? The only answer she could find to that made her pale.

'I don't—Bryna?' Raff looked at her with concern, coming down on his haunches beside her chair as he grasped her suddenly cold hands in his. 'Darling, what is it?'

He sounded so concerned for her. Could it be true? Had she trusted and believed the wrong man?

'Bryna?' Raff sounded desperate now. 'Kate, call the doctor——'

'No,' she managed to choke out. 'I—I think I'd like to go and lie down for a while.' She looked at Raff with darkly purple eyes. 'Would you please help me up the stairs?'

Pleasure blazed in his eyes before it was quickly brought under control. 'Of course.' He stood up to swing her up into his arms.

She didn't protest, not altogether sure her legs would support her weight if she had tried to stand up on her own. 'I'm just tired,' she assured Kate and Roger wryly as they watched her anxiously.

Raff gave them what could only be described as a wolfish grin. 'It's really just her way of dragging me off to bed to have her wicked way with me!' he teased, instantly easing their tension. 'I wish she would realise I'm not going to argue!'

His teasing had eased the atmosphere of worry, although his expression became grim again as he carried Bryna up to her room, placing her down carefully on the bed. 'What happened down there?' he asked gently.

She closed her eyes a moment, breathing deeply to calm her racing thoughts. She had to be wrong. But did she want to be—didn't she want all those horrific accusations that were crashing about in her head to be true so that she was free to love Raff again? She knew, no matter how painful it would be if what she suspected were true, that she *so much* wanted it to be right.

'Raff, who told you about my having an affair with Court?' She looked at him unblinkingly.

'Bryna——'

'Raff, please answer, this is very important to the future of our marriage.' She grasped his arm encouragingly.

'The future of ...?' Suddenly he looked as vulnerable as he had claimed to be earlier. 'Bryna, don't play games with me!'

'I'm not,' she shook her head, still feeling ill. 'But I think someone has been playing a game with us, a sickeningly destructive game!'

'What are you talking about?' he groaned his impatience.

'Raff, did you ask Stuart Hillier to spy on me?'

Anger darkened his face. 'Of course not,' he rasped. 'I'll admit he was the first one to mention seeing you and Court together, but I certainly never asked him to *spy* on you!'

'Then who did?' she probed quietly.

'No one did,' Raff dismissed impatiently. 'You——'

'Then why did he?' she persisted.

'He didn't! He saw you in a couple of restaurants together and just happened to mention it to me——'

'Raff, how many restaurants are there in London?' she reasoned.

He gave a perplexed frown. 'I don't know, hundreds probably,' he shrugged.

'Then how is it that I've been seen so regularly with Court in *different* restaurants, by both you and Stuart Hillier?'

'Coincidence, I suppose——'

'That's exactly what he said,' she recalled flatly.

'He?' Raff looked totally confused. 'You mean Stuart?'

'No—Court.'

Kate said she had seen Court with Stuart Hillier a couple of weeks ago, and yet when Bryna had spoken to Court ten days ago he had trouble remembering the other man's name! She had nothing else to go on but the coincidence of the restaurants, the meeting Kate had witnessed, and Court's memory lapse about the other man's name, and yet suddenly she knew. She *knew*!

'But that sort of coincidence doesn't occur in a place as big as London unless schedules are known and shared,' she sighed. 'Court had been trying to drive a wedge in our relationship almost since it began,' she told Raff dully. 'It has to be him. I

thought it was you, but—but now I know it's Court.'
She swallowed hard, the pain of disillusionment
almost too much to bear. She had genuinely liked
Court, and he had tried to destroy her, had almost
succeeded in destroying her child.

Raff sat on the edge of the bed, frowning darkly.
'How do you know?'

She blinked back the tears. 'For now will you just
accept it if I tell you I *do* know?'

'Darling Bryna, don't you know I would accept it
if you told me black was white and white was
black?'

That was it. The day she had first met Court and
been introduced to Raff she had believed Court was
the light one, like the sun, and Raff was the dark
secretive one, like the moon. She had gone on
thinking of them in that way even after she fell in
love with Raff, and all the time she had had the two
men the wrong way around; Raff was her sunlight,
Court was the dark destructive one.

'He saw exactly what I thought,' she realised
chokingly. 'And that I loved you anyway. And he
used that love against me!'

'You—love—me?'

It was a strangulated plea that it be the truth, and
she looked at Raff with all her love shining in her
eyes for him. 'I've always loved you. I fell in love
with you that first night we went out together, and
it's continued that way. I would never have agreed
to have an affair with you if I hadn't loved you,' she
added ruefully.

He grasped her arms. 'And I never would have

settled for one if I'd known how you felt!' he groaned.

Bryna looked up at him uncertainly. 'What do you mean? The affair was your idea——'

He shook his head. 'Yours.'

'But——'

'We made love, and I was about to tell you how much I loved you and wanted to marry you when you started talking about how clever you'd been to choose someone as skilled as me as your first lover, how we both knew the rules—no ties, no commitment, how we would just enjoy each other,' he remembered bitterly. 'For the first time since my youthful love for Josey I'd been about to bare my soul and tell a woman how much I loved her, and before I could she told me she was only interested in my body! Talk about a reversal of the roles!' The pain he had known could still be heard in his voice.

'I thought it was what you wanted,' she pleaded for his understanding.

'I don't usually take a woman home to meet my children on a second date,' he groaned. 'I fell in love with you almost instantly, couldn't get you of my mind, and that day I returned from my business trip to America and you greeted me like a spitting tigress I knew I had to have you for my wife, that I always wanted you to be there when I came home. But I had other commitments in my life, and I thought it best if you met Kate and Paul so that you knew what those commitments were, if by some miracle I could persuade you to marry me.'

'I didn't know how you felt about me, Raff,' she squeezed his hands in her own. 'But he did. And he used our uncertainty of each other against us.'

'But why?'

'I don't know,' she sighed. 'I wish I did.'

'Bryna, do you really love me?' Raff still didn't
look as if he really believed her.

'So very much,' she said with feeling.

'Then you must have been going through the
same hell I have,' he groaned, his eyes dark with
pain. 'Bryna, I love you. I love you so much!'

'Raff, make love to me,' she urged throatily.

He blinked. 'Now?'

'Don't you want to?' she teased huskily.

He gave her a look that told her just how much.
'But I don't want to hurt you or the baby. We've had
one scare——'

'That had nothing to do with our making love,'
she assured him quickly.

'You almost fainted downstairs just now,' he
reminded her concernedly.

'Both I and the baby would like to be reacquaint-
ed with the man we love!' Her eyes shone, no more
shadows on her love for him.

'If we have a daughter and she looked at me the
way you do I'll never be able to deny her anything!'
he groaned as he buried his face in her hair.

Bryna cradled his head lovingly, for the first time
knowing herself loved in return by this magnificent
man. 'I'll make sure it's a boy so that your authority
won't be threatened,' she teased.

He didn't seem to care very much about that as he
made slow love to her, touching every inch of her,
his hands possessive against their child as he

suckled against her, driving them both towards the edge of fulfilment.

When finally the silken shaft of him was encased inside her they were both so highly aroused that they just lay together as the waves of pleasure washed all the past pain away.

Raff lay damply against her breasts. 'Perhaps it's as well you're already pregnant, otherwise I have a feeling you would be after tonight!'

Bryna knew exactly what he meant. The first time they had ever made love had been so earth-shatteringly perfect, but although they had always found pleasure in each other's arms it had never ben quite that perfect again. Tonight, just now, it had superseded perfection, had been a vow to how much they loved each other. And she now knew why the first time and just now had been so different from all the others; on neither occasion had they tried to hide their love from each other. This time nothing would spoil that.

'I love you, Raff,' she told him softly. 'I'm proud to be carrying your child.'

'No more proud than I am,' his lips moved against her moistly. 'God, we've said some vicious things to each other in an effort to hide our love.' His arms tightened. 'I felt as if you'd twisted a knife inside me the night I had to rush you to hospital and you told me you would never have had *my* child if you'd realised you could ever have had one!'

'Because Court had just told me enough at Kate's dinner party to convince me you had asked Stuart Hillier to spy on me! And because you'd already told me *you* wished I weren't pregnant either!'

'Because of you,' groaned Raff, trembling slightly. 'I thought you were going to die and be taken from me now.' He picked up her left hand, kissing the eternity ring that sat so comfortably next to her wedding ring. 'I could see you were puzzled when I gave you this,' he told her huskily. 'But it means exactly what it's supposed to; I'll love you for eternity. And I can take anything but losing you!'

'You'll never lose me,' Bryna promised fervently. 'Although I can't guarantee that we will ever have another child,' she added uncertainly. 'This one is still a miracle to me.'

'I love the baby because we made it together,' he looked down at her with dark eyes. 'But it isn't something I planned either.'

She frowned. 'Are you sure you want another child in the house?'

'Sure?' he dismissed lightly. 'I'm looking forward to it. When Josey and I had Kate and Paul I was very young, believed it was a woman's place to take care of the babies while I went out and earned the money. I intend being involved in every aspect of this baby!'

'Oh, Raff, I didn't realise, not even once, that you loved me,' she groaned. 'You said you were only marrying me for the baby——'

'Because using the baby was the only way to make sure *you* would marry me,' he corrected. 'At first you seemed happy enough with the affair you asked for, and then you started to drift away from me. I took on Stuart Hillier in the first place in an effort to delegate my work and spend more time with you, showing you how much I needed you——'

'You only seemed to need me in bed, cruelly cut me out of any interest in your work or Kate and Paul——'

'Because I believed the commitment to my work and my grown-up family were part of the reason you only wanted an affair with me,' he shook his head. 'Kate and Paul seemed like a reminder of how much older and more experienced I was than you, and so I did my best to keep the three of you apart. I didn't always succeed, but after that first night when you seemed so lost in their company I certainly tried.'

'It was only that it seemed a little—strange, meeting your children. I *wanted* to share them as the months passed,' Bryna sighed her impatience with the misunderstandings that had kept them apart for so long. 'Your refusal to do so seemed a way of telling me you wanted me in bed but in no other part of your life. And then even that began to pall, be less intense. When you agreed so readily to my condition that we wouldn't sleep together during our marriage I believed you no longer wanted me.'

Raff gave a self-derisive groan. 'I only agreed because I had no intention of being married to you and yet living apart. But the only way I could get you to marry me at all was by using blackmail, and to have told you then that I intended it to be a normal marriage would have frightened you away. I stayed away from you until after we were married, but I never intended to live like that for the rest of our lives.'

'You told me those nights that you only wanted to touch the baby!'

'And you,' he smiled. 'I never intended to let you

go.' He gave a pained frown. 'Until it seemed you preferred Court to me. You told me you were leaving me after he visited you in hospital, and I thought——'

'Alyson visited me too that night,' she frowned. 'She told me she'd been out with Stuart Hillier and he'd asked a lot of questions about me, and I thought it was because of——'

'Me,' Raff realised grimly. 'I didn't put him up to it, so it must have been Court.'

'Raff, we have to talk about Court,' Bryna told him quietly. 'But first of all we have to understand that we love each other, that Court can never use our uncertainty of each other to hurt us again. I don't know why he wanted to hurt us, but I do think a little boy capable of attacking another little boy with a cricket bat and breaking his nose can't have just lost that temper because he's now an adult. He may be able to control it better, but not to lose it completely.

'Court told you about that episode when we were at school together?' Raff frowned.

'The first day we met,' she nodded. 'Oh, it's obvious he's a controlled man now, but that vindictiveness must still be below that surface pleasantness. We have to be sure of our love for each other before we challenge him on it, have no doubts, otherwise he'll still be able to find a way to drive us apart.'

'Darling Bryna, I swear to you I will never doubt you or your love again,' he looked down at her with dark eyes. 'It was only because I loved you so much and it didn't seem to be returned that I've been acting like a madman since we got married, throwing out accusations while still secretly hoping we could start again and make our marriage work. That day I saw you lunching with Court and made that threat to you about forcing our marriage to be a real one I was so disgusted with myself by the time I got back to my office that I felt too sickened to come home at all that night. I dreaded coming home to find that you'd left me, acted like an idiot again when I found that you hadn't.'

She could see that Court had been able to witness their weakness about each other all the time, and that he had used that to hurt them. But she didn't doubt Raff's love now; she knew that all his cruelty since they were married had been because his heart was breaking and he just didn't know what to do to hold on to her. He would never have *reason* to doubt her love for him again.

'Call Court and ask him to come over,' she said huskily.

'Now?' Raff's eyes widened.

'It isn't that late, and this can't wait any longer,' she insisted dully. 'We have to know *why*, Raff.'

He had barely had time to get out of bed and pull on his trousers before a knock sounded on the bedroom door.

Kate stood outside, her amused gaze going from her father's tousled appearance to Bryna's blushing cheeks. 'And I thought you were joking downstairs,' she mocked. 'I came to say goodnight, but that seems a little——'

'Kate!' her father warned.

'See you both in the morning. Or afternoon,' she

added cheekily. 'I guess the honeymoon isn't over!'

Raff gave a rueful smile as he closed the door behind her. 'She isn't going to let us forget this in a hurry!'

Bryna laughed softly, her eyes glowing with pleasure as she watched the ripple of muscles across his shoulders as he dressed. 'She'll have to get used to it.'

His eyes softened caressingly. 'God, I hope so!'

'You can be sure of it,' she promised huskily.

'I never told you, but I felt so damned grateful that I was the first man to make love to you,' long fingers caressed her cheek. 'I was going to tell you, but——'

'I started talking about rules and no commitment,' she realised ruefully. 'I thought it was what you wanted!'

'You were still a virgin because you were afraid, weren't you?' he said huskily. 'Afraid you were incomplete in some way?'

'Yes,' she nodded with remembered sadness. 'I'd like to say I saved myself for you, but the truth is——'

'The truth is that was exactly what you did,' he finished firmly. 'I'm sure I wasn't the first man to want to make love to you, and yet it was *me* you trusted to make you feel you were a complete woman.'

'I loved you,' she said simply. 'I needed you.'

'We'll always need each other, Bryna. I promise you nothing else will drive us apart!' he vowed fiercely.

When Raff telephoned Court the other man had

just got in, although he was obviously alone, but he
agreed to come over straight away.

Bryna and Raff were seated together on the sofa
when the doorbell rang a short time later. Raff went
to answer the door himself, having dismissed the
staff for the night, and Kate obviously having gone
to bed and to sleep too.

Court was still wearing the evening suit he had
obviously worn to go out in. He gave Bryna a
friendly nod, refusing Raff's invitation for him to sit
down. He turned to the other man. 'So what was so
important it couldn't wait until morning?'

'Did you have a pleasant evening?' Raff enquired
cordially, handing him a glass of brandy.

Court gave a puzzled frown. 'Very nice, thank
you,' he answered distractedly. 'What——'

'See anyone we know while you were out, my
assistant, for instance?' Raff added, silky-soft.

Court's eyes widened. 'Hillier?' he queried. 'Why
should I have seen him?'

'Well, you look as if you've probably eaten out
this evening, and with the coincidental meetings
that have gone on at restaurants lately I wondered if
the two of you might have met.' Raff quirked dark
brows, his eyes icy.

Court glanced at Bryna's stony expression, and
then back to Raff's accusing one, giving a choked
cry as he dropped down into an armchair. 'I never
meant it to go this far,' he groaned, his face buried
in his hands.

Bryna looked at Raff in stunned disbelief; the last
thing either of them had expected had been an
instant confession from Court. In fact, she was sure

that secretly they had both hoped they had made some terrible mistake. But that was impossible now, and some of the coldness drained out of Bryna as she saw how broken Court was.

'Why, Court?' Raff prompted gruffly, and Bryna wanted to go to him and comfort him because of the pain she knew he was suffering. But she sat completely still, having the feeling this was something the two men had to settle between them. The time to comfort Raff would be after Court had gone.

'Because I loved her and she wouldn't leave you!' Tears fell unashamedly down Court's cheeks. 'I was okay to go to bed with, even to love a little, but she wouldn't leave *you!*'

Bryna gasped. 'I never went to bed with you——'

'Not you,' Court shook his head. 'Josey!' he explained bitterly. 'We were lovers for five years before she died, and although I pleaded with her, *begged* her, to leave Raff, she never would.'

Bryna could plainly see what a shock this revelation was to Raff. Of course he had always known there was someone else in Josey's life, but not Court!

'I couldn't give her the children she wanted if she left you,' Court continued harshly. 'And she knew you would never let her take Kate and Paul away from you. I waited ten years for you to love someone the way I loved Josey,' his eyes glittered as he glared at Raff. 'And when Bryna did come along you were too damned arrogant to tell her how you felt.'

Raff drew in a ragged breath. 'And you used that to hurt me.'

'It was what I wanted—I wanted you to know

how I felt, loving Josey but unable to have her,' Court rasped. 'Unfortunately Bryna got hurt too, and I didn't plan on that happening, I really do like her. When she almost lost the baby I knew I had to stop. I could never hurt an unborn child, never hurt any child!'

'And Hillier?' Raff frowned. 'Where does he come into all this?'

Court's mouth twisted. 'I should get rid of him, Raff—he can be bought!'

'I loved you like a brother, Court,' Raff groaned his pain.

'I loved you the same way,' the other man nodded. 'But as soon as I saw Josey I fell in love with her. Remember the first time we saw her, Raff?' he smiled. 'It was at a party given by my parents. I thought she was the most beautiful woman I'd ever seen. But she only saw you,' he added flatly.

'I had no idea you felt that way about her . . .!' Raff shook his head.

'Why should you?' Court gave a self-derisive smile. 'You couldn't help the fact that women always preferred you. And with the others it never mattered,' he added grimly. 'I thought your relationship with her would run its usual course and then I could help her pick up the pieces, only she became pregnant before that happened, and I had to resign myself to just being a friend to you all. But the marriage never worked, did it, Raff, and after a couple of years you were both looking around for other people. I hung around until Josey eventually turned to me. But I couldn't give her the children she so desperately wanted!'

'Maybe if the two of you had come to me, talked to me about taking Kate and Paul——'

'What?' challenged Court. 'You would have let us have them?' he scorned.

Raff drew in a ragged breath. 'Maybe,' he breathed huskily.

'You would never have agreed——'

'I might have done,' Raff protested. 'It would have been hard for me, but I knew how much Josey loved them, and that you loved them too.'

Court looked at him angrily. 'You can't bring yourself to hate me even now, can you?' he choked.

'I could try, if you really want me to,' Raff told him raggedly.

'I nearly drove you and Bryna apart, nearly killed your baby!'

Raff nodded. 'And if you'd succeeded in doing either of those things maybe I could hate you. But I've loved you as a brother too long to hate you for what might have been.'

Bryna loved Raff more in that moment than ever before, as she went to his side to clutch his hand tightly. They had both suffered because of Court, but Raff had suffered much more than she, would probably always suffer for the loss of a man he had felt so close to.

Court stood up in controlled movements. 'Since I went to see Bryna in hospital I've spent the time moving my head office to New York,' he told them tautly. 'I intended telling you what I'd done before I left, but as soon as my move has been completed I'll be going to the States myself. Unless you have other plans for me?' He looked enquiringly at Raff.

Raff's arm moved about Bryna's waist as he drew her close to his side. 'You've done nothing illegal. And even if you had I doubt I would want to do anything about it.'

Court sighed. 'Then I'll say goodbye; I doubt we'll meet again.' He looked regretfully at Bryna. 'I really am sorry you almost lost the baby.'

'I know you are,' she nodded.

As soon as the front door had closed behind him Bryna felt Raff sag weakly against her, turning towards him as he sobbed in her arms.

'If you don't stop picking him up every time he so much as squeaks he's going to be thoroughly spoilt!' Bryna scolded as she walked into the nursery.

Raff turned guiltily, the tiny baby held securely in his arms. 'I thought he was choking.'

Bryna firmly took the baby away from him and put him back in his crib, ignoring the indignant wails that followed them as she pulled Raff from the room. 'Correction,' she said sternly. 'He's already spoilt!'

James Rafferty Gallagher—the reversal of the two first names Bryna had originally chosen had come about because Raff had decided they couldn't have two Raffertys in the house—was almost seven weeks old, but he had known from the day Bryna brought him home five weeks ago that *he* was going to be master in this house. With his thickly curling dark hair and purple eyes he charmed on sight!

'He was crying——'

'He's been changed, fed, cuddled, and now he needs to sleep. He just doesn't think he does,' she added firmly as Raff went to protest. 'Honestly, I sometimes wish that new assistant of yours wasn't so good at his job that you don't feel the need to put in more than the odd day or so at your office!'

But they both knew she wished nothing of the sort. She and Raff were together almost continuously, and they loved it. Raff's new assistant really was very good, and after taking over again during the latter part of Bryna's pregnancy, Alyson was running the agency very smoothly too.

'Between you, Kate and Paul, I hardly ever get to hold James myself,' Bryna complained, knowing she was really pleased by the acceptance of *all* the family of the baby that could have been an intrusion. But Kate and Paul were always here to see James, and on the odd occasion when Bryna and Raff went out for the evening they usually argued over which one of them was going to come over and babysit. Kate had moved during the summer to share a flat with another girl from college, and fortunately it seemed to be working out this time.

Both Kate and Paul had been upset by their 'uncle's' move to America, and Bryna knew that Raff often thought of Court too. But from pieces of information Raff received Court seemed to be doing well in the States, and now that their own happiness was so overflowing they wished him well. Maybe one day he would even find a woman he could love as much as he had Josey.

'Stop trying to find reasons to pick an argument with me and tell me what the doctor said this morning,' Raff encouraged throatily.

After the way he had been storming frustratedly about the house the last couple of months she had been deeply disappointed at his lack of interest earlier in her visit to the doctor for her post-natal check-up. Looking at him now, his eagerness barely contained, she realised he had been trying to be tactful, not wanting to pressure her.

She gave him a seductive smile. 'As soon as your son is asleep I'll tell you,' she ran caressing fingers down his cheek, his face softened with love for her.

He listened in the direction of the nursery, giving her a triumphant look as silence greeted them. 'Who said he was spoilt?' he drawled pointedly.

She laughed softly, moving into his arms. 'Who insisted he be put back in his crib?'

'You planned this,' Raff groaned. 'Oh God, Bryna, I've missed your closeness, missed being a part of you!'

'You'll always be a part of me,' she looked at him lovingly. 'I love you.'

'I love you too!'

They told each other of their feelings all the time now, not just after the loving but before and during too. It would always be that way for them now.

Harlequin Presents

Coming Next Month

1023 TOO SHORT A BLESSING Penny Jordan
After the tragic death of her fiancé, a young Englishwoman becomes convinced that she'll never fall in love again—until she meets a very determined man who has every intention of changing her mind...and reaching her heart.

1024 MASQUERADE MARRIAGE Flora Kidd
On a Caribbean cruise, Carlotta discovers that the deckhand paying so much attention to her is really a bodyguard hired by her wealthy father because of kidnapping threats. The complication of their falling in love is not part of the plan.

1025 CIRCLE OF FATE Charlotte Lamb
Things get complicated when Melanie, already doubtful about her engagement to a prominent businessman, meets another man who infuriates her, but also attracts her. Breaking off her engagement, however, doesn't immediately bring about the desired results!

1026 A RACY AFFAIR Roberta Leigh
Emma Fielding, governess to a racing car driver's motherless child, is persuaded to marry him so there'll be a guardian in case of his death. When they fall in love with each other, they're too afraid at first to admit it.

1027 OUT OF THE SHADOWS Sandra Marton
When Lauren meets the man she knows is right for her, past bitterness between their families threatens their love. Can they selfishly ignore the hurtful consequences of their actions to achieve a happy future together?

1028 BRITTANY'S CASTLE Leigh Michaels
Successful banker Brittany Masters reluctantly agrees to a mock reconciliation with her unfaithful husband until he obtains a government appointment. In return he'll give her a divorce. The situation is awkward, but happily nothing turns out as they expect.

1029 NO STRINGS ATTACHED Annabel Murray
When lively, actively social, travel agent Vita, believing in love and commitment, meets attractive but footloose Dominic, looking for a temporary affair, conflict is inevitable. So, too, is love—but in between is a time of turmoil.

1030 TOUCH AND GO Elizabeth Oldfield
That it turns out to be a hoax, doesn't make her stepfather's kidnapping any less harrowing for Karis, visiting him in Bangkok. Especially when the only one she can turn to is the man she'd loved and broken off with six months before.

Available in November wherever paperback books are sold, or through Harlequin Reader Service:

In the U.S.
901 Fuhrmann Blvd.
P.O. Box 1397
Buffalo, N.Y. 14240-1397

In Canada
P.O. Box 603
Fort Erie, Ontario
L2A 5X3

Can you keep a secret?

You can keep this one plus 4 free novels

What readers say about Harlequin romance fiction...

"I absolutely adore Harlequin romances! They are fun and relaxing to read, and each book provides a wonderful escape."
–N.E.,* Pacific Palisades, California

"Harlequin is the best in romantic reading."
–K.G.,* Philadelphia, Pennsylvania

"Harlequins have been my passport to the world. I have been many places without ever leaving my doorstep."
–P.Z.,* Belvedere, Illinois

"My praise for the warmth and adventure your books bring into my life."
–D.F.,*Hicksville, New York

"A pleasant way to relax after a busy day."
–P.W.,* Rector, Arkansas

*Names available on request.

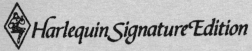
Harlequin Signature Edition

Penny Jordan

Stronger Than Yearning

He was the man of her dreams!

The same dark hair, the same mocking eyes; it was as if the
Regency rake of the portrait, the seducer of Jenna's dream, had
come to life. Jenna, believing the last of the Deverils dead, was
determined to buy the great old Yorkshire Hall—to claim it for
her daughter, Lucy, and put to rest some of the painful memories of Lucy's birth. She had no way of knowing that a direct des-
cendant of the black sheep Deveril even existed—or that James
Allingham and his own powerful yearnings would disrupt her
plan entirely.

Penny Jordan's first Harlequin Signature Edition *Love's Choices* was an
outstanding success. Penny Jordan has written more than 40 best-sell-
ing titles—more than 4 million copies sold.

Now, be sure to buy her latest bestseller, *Stronger Than Yearning*. Available wherever paperbacks are sold—in October.

Six exciting series
for you every month...
from Harlequin

Harlequin Romance·
The series that started it all

Tender, captivating and heartwarming...
love stories that sweep you off to faraway places
and delight you with the magic of love.

Harlequin Presents·
Powerful contemporary love
stories...as individual as the
women who read them

The No. 1 romance series...
exciting love stories for you, the woman of today...
a rare blend of passion and dramatic realism.

Harlequin Superromance®
It's more than romance...
it's Harlequin Superromance

A sophisticated, contemporary romance-fiction
series, providing you with a longer,
more involving read...a richer mix of complex plots,
realism and adventure.

Harlequin
American Romance™
Harlequin celebrates the American woman...

...by offering you romance stories written about American women, by American women for American women. This series offers you contemporary romances uniquely North American in flavor and appeal.

◆

Harlequin Temptation
Passionate stories for today's woman

An exciting series of sensual, mature stories of love...dilemmas, choices, resolutions... all contemporary issues dealt with in a true-to-life fashion by some of your favorite authors.

◆

Harlequin Intrigue
Because romance can be quite an adventure

Harlequin Intrigue, an innovative series that blends the romance you expect... with the unexpected. Each story has an added element of intrigue that provides a new twist to the Harlequin tradition of romance excellence.

Harlequin Books·

PROD-A-2

Harlequin Intrigue
Adopts a New Cover Story!

**We are proud to present to you
the new Harlequin Intrigue cover design.**

Look for these exciting new stories, which mix a contemporary, sophisticated romance with the surprising twists and turns of a puzzler . . . romance with "something more."

Plus . . . we are also offering you the chance to enter the Intrigue Mystery Weekend Sweepstakes in the October Intrigue titles. Win one of four mysterious and romantic weekends.

Buy the October Harlequin Intrigues!